to my childhood

Jeff Carlanen

Hog Hollow

By

Jeff Cavaness

1663 LIBERTY DRIVE, SUITE 200
BLOOMINGTON, INDIANA 47403
(800) 839-8640
WWW.AUTHORHOUSE.COM

This book is a work of fiction. People, places, events, and situations are the product of the author's imagination. Any resemblance to actual persons, living or dead, or historical events, is purely coincidental.

© *2005 Jeff Cavaness. All Rights Reserved.*

No part of this book may be reproduced, stored in a retrieval system, or transmitted by any means without the written permission of the author.

First published by AuthorHouse 02/23/05

ISBN: 1-4208-3297-2 (sc)

Library of Congress Control Number: 2005901408

*Printed in the United States of America
Bloomington, Indiana*

This book is printed on acid-free paper.

To Jane: for always being supportive

To Adam: for wanting to hear

I dedicate this book to you with love.

TABLE OF CONTENTS

HOG HOLLOW 1

RILEY 3

THE GOOSE 7

STUMP TALKING 11

MY DOG, MY PROTECTOR 17

MY FIRST TEDDY BEAR OR MY 1ST STORE-BOUGHT TEDDY BEAR 21

STOP THOSE CHICKENS FROM FIGHTING 25

THE BLACK ROPE 29

THE TUNNEL 33

I DON'T LIKE PINK RABBITS 43

LISTEN TO THE BIRDS 47

THE COCKER SPANIEL 51

THE WILLOW TREE 55

BREEDING CATTLE AIN'T GOOD SUPPER
TABLE TALK 61

MISS CONNIE AND THE FISH 69

REGGIE AND THE MAMA PIG 75

PARTY LINE 83

THE GRAVEYARD 87

FRONTIER CAMPFIRE 91

THE TRUTH COMES OUT 95

REGGIE AND OLD MAN PALMER 101

THE FIRE AND THE CHICKENS 113

I HATE SNAKES 119

PLUCKING CHICKENS 123

THE BACK PORCH SNAKE 127

MY DUCK 131

THE COW AND THE ELECTRIC FENCE 135

TYLER'S STORE 141

PLAYING IN THE FLOOD 145

SLEEPY HOLLOW	149
GRASSHOPPER	163
THE CAR WRECK	171
HALLOWEEN	179
THE TRAILOR PARK	183
CAMPING	191
THE GOATS	195
LOVERS' LANE	201
THE SCIENCE FAIR	205
THE CHRISTMAS PLAY	211
THE PIG FARMER AND THE DEBUTANTE	217
SURPRISE! I'M A FARM BOY	221
MEMORIES OF THE FARM	225
HOG HOLLER REVISITED	231
ABOUT THE AUTHOR	235

HOG HOLLOW

I grew up in Hog Hollow but to be correct you have to say "Hog Holler". To be perfectly honest, the real name was Standfield Chapel. "Hog Holler" was just what everyone for miles around called where we lived. The reason for this was that most of the folks abouts raise hogs. Hog Holler was a great place to live, if you liked hogs.

Jeff Cavaness

RILEY

My name is Riley Washington Standfield. Ain't you impressed? I hope so. I sure wasn't growing up. I just wondered why I couldn't have a name like everybody else; you know, like Bill, Tom or Pete. Anyway, my names, Riley and Washington are family names, sort of. Riley was my great-granddaddy's name and everyone born into our family is named after someone famous. I had uncles named after presidents, prophets, you know, anybody who had their name in a book. I'll let you guess where the Washington comes from. I once asked my granddaddy what our last name meant. He looked at me and said, "It means man standing out in the field." I never knew if he was serious or what.Growing up in Hog Holler was very cocoonish. (Ain't that a great word? I just love words. I sometimes like to make up my own words. You will probably see some if you ain't already.) I was kin to almost everybody who lived there. In fact, the church was even named for my family, Standfield Chapel Presbyterian Church. One of my ancestor kin donated the land for the church and the cemetery. Being that the majority of all the congregation was in some way connected with our family, it's not too hard to understand how they come up that the name.

Being surrounded by family has its ups and downs. It is a safe place to grow up and it's fun to be able to know so much about your family. (If you don't know much about your family, why don't you ask one of your older kin? I be they would love to tell you about your great-uncle Elmer or your cousin Minnie Faye.) Anyway, I can tell you who my ninth cousin is and stuff like that. One of the downs was when we were at church. If I ever did something I shouldn't of my mother heard about it two dozen times before I even had a chance to think of some reason I did what I knew I shouldn't of been doing. I just couldn't get away with nothing. At times like those I just knew I had way too many kin. To let you kinda know what I'm talking about having too many kin, we lived about seven miles outside of town. About one mile out of town you passed over the Standfield line; you know, the point of no return. From there on, on both sides of the road everyone's house you passed was either as Standfield or someone kin to the Standfields'.

Because of this, I got into trouble with my driving several times. When I finally got my drivers' license I'd be coming back from town or wherever; and if'n I went around a curve too fast, (I would

Jeff Cavaness

regret it.) and let me tell you, we had lots of curves and twists in the road. (My friends from school used to say Daniel Boone would get lost trying to find our house.) Did I tell you I'm descended from Daniel Boone. We got an old family Bible. In that Bible is written the entire family way, way back. Anyway, Daniel Boone's granddaughter, Nycie, married into my family. What do you think about that!

Back to my driving, if I turned a curve just a little too fast, my mother had heard about it ten times before I ever got home. Once I tried coming home a different way, it didn't matter, I was surrounded by kin.

Remember what I said about too many kin, it was times like that that I wondered what it would be like to not have any relatives.

THE GOOSE

I want to go on record by saying, "I hate gooses, geese, whatever." I hated one goose in particular. When I was about 5 or 6 one of my cousins, a city cousin at that, brought my mother a goose. He had gotten it when it was a chick or whatever they call baby gooses and now that is was growed up, he didn't have a place for it. He thought that since we had a farm, it would be the perfect place for it.

Jeff Cavaness

(He should of asked my opinion.)

Well, anyway, one day he shows up with this goose for my mother. My mother was tickled. She was tickled because she knew she wouldn't have to take care of it. It was decided that because it was just one goose, it wouldn't be too much trouble and I could see to it.

Do you know anything about gooses? Well, let me tell you. They ain't nice. They are foul tempered and they smell bad too. Ours must have been King Goose because he was the meanest and stinkiest goose I've ever been around.

The first thing that goose did was bite me on the butt. Remember, I was 5 or 6 so I wasn't that much taller than this big ole goose. And biting me on the butt did not help my feelings about it either. I couldn't to nothing to it because I'd get in trouble. Needless to say, I didn't want to be around it much. I was always scared it would bite me again.

It wasn't long after the goose came to live with us that one of our cats tried to have King Goose for dinner. It didn't succeed but you would thought the world was coming to an end with all the racket and commotion that was going on. After that we had to build a pen for the goose to protect it from the cats. (Guess who got to stand guard!)

"Riley, you got to keep watch over that goose. The cat'll get it if you don't?"

"And that's a problem, Mama." To me the cat getting the goose was a good thing. Let the cat have it as far as I was concerned.

"Riley." Mama looked me hard.

"Okay, okay." I was not happy. Babysitting a mean stinky goose was not my idea of a fun time.

So the days went by with my standing watch over the goose and the goose trying his best to bite my butt any chance he got. One day after school I went out to see to the goose and found the pen was empty. I looked and looked; well, not too hard, but I did look. I was afraid I would get blamed if something happened to that goose. Personally, I was about ready to accept any punishment as long I didn't have tend to that mean smelly bird any longer.

I did honestly try to find the goose but I couldn't. I even tried to find some feathers from where some cat or some other varmint may have gotten it but I found nothing. I did decided to not say anything. Maybe no one would notice it was gone. I went about my chores and playing until I heard my mother calling me in for supper. I washed up and went in and sat down at the table. I looked up and saw my mother coming to the table with a big plate of chicken. It looked and smelled great!

"Mama, when did you kill this chicken? I didn't hear you out back."

She looked at me and smiled real big. "Riley, this is not chicken."

I looked at her and then back at the chicken and suddenly what had happened dawned on me.

You know, that was the best supper I have ever had!

STUMP TALKING

Have you ever heard the expression; "He could talk to a stump!"? That expression got started in my family. Actually, it got started because of me.

Let me start at the beginning. My family was big hunters. When I was about 5 years old my daddy took me squirrel hunting. It was exciting for a little boy to be with his daddy out in the woods all alone.

Jeff Cavaness

As we were walking along I was acting like a perfectly normal little 5-year-old boy, I was talking. I was asking questions about the squirrels, the trees and anything else that popped into my head. My daddy would answer quietly and continue to look in the trees. This went on for the better part of an hour until we reached a clearing in the woods. In the center was a big stump. More than likely an old tree had fallen and left this clearing and the rest of the woods had not filled in the gaps yet.

Anyway, when I saw the stump I ran and jumped up on top of it and started jumping around and just talking away. My daddy looked at me and then walked over to the stump.

"Riley, why don't just stay here on this stump while I go look for the squirrels a little longer."

"Daddy, no, I want to go with you." I wasn't scared of being left alone in the woods. I just wanted to be with my daddy.

"No, you stay and rest. I'm just gonna be right over yonder in those trees."

I stayed. I didn't have any choice. When my

daddy said something, you usually needed to do as he said without too much argument. So I stayed on the stump and looked around at the woods to see what or if anything was interesting to look at. Being bored with that real quick, I started talking.

Let me explain something right here before I go any farther. I had a brother but he was much older so I never really had anyone to play with on a regular-like basis. Oh, occasionally a cousin or a friend might come over but usually I had to entertain myself. One of the ways I did that was to tell myself stories. I guess I started very young. One other part to this is that I love to talk. I liked talking when I was 5 and I still like doing it now even though I'm considerably older. Well, let me finish my story.

I got to talking to entertain myself and really never worried about being out there by myself. As I got older, I never was much of a hunter but I loved being out in the fields and woods. I used to roam and look and listen. To me, being outside where everything was fresh and clean and quiet was pure enjoyment. Plus, being 5 years old, I wasn't old enough to know that being all alone in the woods can be dangerous under the wrong circumstances.

As I was sitting there I heard two big gun shots. "I hope that was my daddy." I started looking around toward the sound of those shots and in a few minutes here my daddy comes holding two dead squirrels.

"Riley, you ready to go?"

"Sure, I'm ready."

We walk back to the truck and go home. Now I'll tell you why this story is important. When we got home, my mother asked how the hunting trip went and I was telling her what happened about the squirrels and about me sitting in the middle of woods on the stump. When I told her about being on the stump all alone my mother looked at my daddy.

"Why did you leave him all alone on that stump?"

My daddy looked at me and smiled. "Because

he was chattering more than the squirrels so I decided the only way to get any was to leave him on that stump and I would go hunt somewhere where it was quieter."

I didn't know this was the true reason for leaving my on that stump. I started to say something but my mother beat me to it.

"Do you think that was very smart doing that, leaving a 5 year old out there all by himself?"

My daddy looked at me and then back at my mother. "Don't worry, I don't think he missed me too much. I would check on him every once in a while and he was there just sitting on that stump and talking."

"Son, who were you talking to out there all by yourself?"

By now, my little 5 year old feelings have been hurt and I look at my daddy and mother and blurt out, "I was talking to the stump!"

They both burst out laughing.

Jeff Cavaness

NOTE: Years later after I got married I told my wife that story and she didn't think it was funny either.

MY DOG, MY PROTECTOR

I want to tell you about a memory of my mother's that's about me, a dog and a snake. As you read my writings you can see that snakes are mentioned several times. It didn't dawn on me until I was grown that this incident probably colored my attitude towards snakes in general.

My father trained coonhound hunting dogs. That was for all you city people. Around where

Jeff Cavaness

I lived anyone who said "coonhound" everyone would know a dog used to hunt coons. Actually, these dogs were used to hunt 'coons, squirrels and anything a hunter might want. My father trained our dogs to hunt 'coons and squirrels primarily.

Another most important quality of these coonhounds was that they could be tremendously loyal to their masters. We even had some dogs that bonded so closely with us they became unsaleable. This did not make my father very happy. If he couldn't sell dogs, no money was made. This happening also caused dogs to be sold more quickly at times. This sometimes caused me great pain because many times I would get attached to a puppy or dog and my father would sell it.

One dog in particular was named Lucy. Lucy was a mostly black with a few white spots hound. She was born on my birthday. Right away she was special. I was able to keep her for about two years before my father sold her. I was heartbroken.

Anyway, this story is not about Lucy. This

story is really not my memory at all because I am too young to remember. One afternoon I was out playing in our front yard. I loved playing in my sandpile. At the time we apparently had a coonhound that was fiercely loyal and protective of me. My mother says that that dog knew exactly when I left the house because he would show up by my side and stay with me until I went back inside the house.

On this particular day I was out playing in my sandpile and my protector was right there with me. My mother was inside working feeling confident that I would be okay. As she was working she heard me start to scream. She heard the dog barking at the same time. With me screaming and the dog barking she knew something was going on that wasn't good. Listening to the screaming and barking intensifying my mother ran to the front porch. What she saw, she says, made her heart start jumping even more. While I had been playing in my sandpile with my protector beside me, a water moccasin had crawled up close to the

Jeff Cavaness

sandpile. (For those of you who may not know, a water moccasin is one of our country's most deadiest snakes.) My dog immediately went into protection and kill mode.

If you didn't know, dogs can and will kill snakes. My dog was no different. He jumped on that snake and by the time my mother got to me the snake was dead. My mother and father examined my dog but could not find anywhere the snake had got him. We watched him for days but he was all right.

You know, that was one dog that was never sold.

MY FIRST TEDDY BEAR OR MY 1ˢᵀ STORE-BOUGHT TEDDY BEAR

I loved animals as a little boy and still do as an adult. One my most favorite things to do even today is go to the zoo. Now it takes on a special quality because I'm sharing the zoo and my feelings about animals with my son. I also loved stuffed animals. I had all kinds and my son now loves his "friends" as he calls them. My mother made stuffed animals to sell to people and my brother and I always got the first two she made of any new stuffed toy. I didn't care. I liked them and would play with them occasionally but mostly I just liked looking at them.

I want to tell you about my very first teddy bear. But first, let me describe our house when I was five years old.

Our house has been added onto many times but the original house had only four rooms, a living room, kitchen and two bedrooms. (No bathroom.) We relied on a wood burning stove for heat and because of that we changed the living room and one of the bedrooms back and forth in the wintertime. My parents didn't want anyone sleeping in the same room with the stove and besides, we had electric blankets for the beds. At Christmas time we would put the Christmas tree in the room without the stove so that meant the Christmas tree was in one of the bedrooms.

Now this was my parents' bedroom but this

particular Christmas Eve I ended up in the bed with my mother and my daddy in the bed with my brother. I don't really remember why. It could have been because I didn't want to sleep with my brother or the other way around. Remember, it's Christmas Eve and most five year olds are very excited. I was no exception. Remember, my brother was older so it could have been he complained about me not settling down enough for him to go to sleep. Who knows! I don't know how Santa Claus got into that room with me sleeping only a few feet away from the tree but he did. On Christmas morning I woke up very early. It was not even close to being light outside. I looked over at that tree and there underneath it was a beautiful brown teddy bear. My mother let me jump out of bed and get the bear and then get back into bed for a while. It was wonderful snuggling under the warm covers with my new friend.

You know, I don't have a clue what else I got that Christmas. I just remember that teddy bear. You know, I still have that bear. It is sitting on top of my son's bookshelf in his room. He can't get to it up there. Sitting next to it is another white teddy bear that my wife had gotten when she was a little girl. I like to think they are sitting up there keeping watch over our son. Occasionally our son will ask to see them which means he wants to hold them. One of us will get them down and he will hold and hug them for a while but they always go back up there to keep watch and to keep young hands at bay.

That little teddy bear is old and worn today. But it represents a very special moment in my life. It is a nice, warm moment for me to remember. I hope you all have some nice, warm moments to remember for yourself.

STOP THOSE CHICKENS FROM FIGHTING

Living on the farm you see all kinds of animal behavior and I saw all of them. But one behavior just still has my brain fuddled.

We had chickens, some, not a lot. My grandparents had lots of chickens. They used to sell the eggs. Chickens are funny creatures. If you never have watched one for very long. You need

Jeff Cavaness

to. They can do some of the strangest things you ever saw. I remember the first time I observed what I thought was "chickens fighting".

I was at my Aunt Rosie's house outside playing. Now, Uncle Linus and Aunt Rosie had turkeys. They were the only ones of the Standfields' that had turkeys. Did you know that turkeys are some of the ugliest birds you have ever seen? Don't get me wrong, I love to eat turkey, but they are ugly. All of a sudden two chickens started flying around and fighting and making all kinds of racket. I ran in the house and told Aunt Rosie.

"Aint Rosie, you got to come do something!"

She could see I was upset.

"What's wrong, Riley?"

"It's your chickens. Something's wrong with two of 'em!"

Aunt Rosie and I hurried out and I took her where the chickens were fighting. They were still at it. The only difference was that my now one of them was on top of the other.

"There they are. There, you see."

Aunt Rosie looked at the chickens and looked at me.

"Riley, what do you want me to do?

"Aint Rosie, stop those chickens from fighting!"

I was about to get upset because Aunt Rosie didn't seem to care that one of her chickens was getting hurt.

"Riley, come on back inside and leave them alone."

"Aint Rosie, why won't you do something?"

Aunt Rosie just smiled and led me back in the house. We went into the kitchen and she fixed me a snack and we both sat down at the kitchen table.

"Riley, those chickens weren't fighting."

"Well, if'n they weren't fighting, what were they doing?"

Aunt Rosie looked a little uncomfortable now that I think about it but then I didn't notice.

"Riley, those chickens were……….Riley, those chickens were mating."

"What!"

"They have to do that to have baby chicks. I can't believe with all the chickens on your place and your granddaddy's that you have never seen that before."

"Well, I haven't. And I don't like it. It shouldn't be so violent."

Aunt Rosie just smiled and got up and went about her business. I, on the other hand, sat there for a few minutes just thinking. You know, I don't care what anybody says, they should,

"Stop those chickens from fighting!"

THE BLACK ROPE

Do you ever remember doing something totally stupid sometime in your life? If you say no, I don't want to say something negative to you but I think you're lying to yourself. We all do stuff that is stupid from time to time. The important aspect of any stupid experience is that we learn from you it, right?

Anyway, one of my earliest stupid experiences

was when I was around 4 years old. You notice that I said, "one of my stupid experiences". I had gone with my daddy over to one of our farms to check on whatever, I didn't know or care at 4 years old. I was just excited to be out wandering around with my daddy.

We checked on the pigs, (Yes, we had pigs everywhere.), and on the cows. Sometimes we had to walk a ways to find those cows. They moved around and while most of the time my daddy knew just where to find them, occasionally even he had a tough time. Today was such a day. We walked and walked but actually I had fun. We were walking around and the day was great and I had a great time.

Now, remember I'm only 4 and while I probably thought I was smart I still had a lot to learn, especially about nature and its animals. We were walking along and we took a short cut through one of our cotton fields. The cotton stalks were about knee level to my daddy which meant they came up to my waist at least. As we were walking along with me chattering away and my daddy occasionally getting a word in edgewise I stopped and pointed toward the end of one of the cotton rows.

"Look Daddy, look at the black rope! I want it!"

I started hurrying toward the black rope. I wanted to play with it. It was several feet long. It would make a great thing to play with.

"Riley, stop! That's not a black rope." He grabbed me from behind.

I stopped and turned back to look at my daddy. "What do you mean it's not a rope? What is it?"

"Watch!"

My daddy bent down and picked up a dirt clod and threw it at the black rope. He hit the black rope at about the midpoint. You know what, that black rope started wriggling and scooted away as fast as it could.

If you haven't figured it out yet, the black rope was a snake. It was what we called a black racer. I told you it was stupid experience. My family got several big laughs out of that one. But like I said, it's not so stupid if you learn something from the experience. I did. I learned to never point out in advance of what I'm doing.

THE TUNNEL

I've told you I have an older brother, Carter. I want to tell you about Carter and our cousin, Mitch. Mitch was a year older than Carter and they were friends and hung around together playing and later getting into all kinds of trouble. (Not real trouble, just boy trouble that makes parents just shake their heads and wonder.)

Carter and Mitch one day decided they would

dig a tunnel. I guess they were bored. Remember, there was not a lot to do in Hog Holler. (I, myself, had a great and extensive imagination (Ha!) and even I, at times, got bored.)

Anyway, they decided to dig this tunnel from one side of this small hill to the other. Actually, I guess it wasn't exactly a hill but that's the best I can describe it for you. They decided to dig so they got some shovels and began to dig. I watched from a safe distance. The digging was not exactly dangerous but sometimes, brothers being brothers and cousins being cousins, Carter and Mitch liked to tease me and chase me and tickle me among other things. I was only 6 so I probably would have been in the way anyway but I was curious to see just exactly what they were doing.

Carter and Mitch dug and dug and finally it actually started looking like a big hole in the ground. My Daddy was not so excited about it as my brother was but since they were not digging in any of the pig lots, he didn't say much. Carter still had his chores to do and as long as the digging didn't interfere with that, I guess Daddy didn't mind.

They dug and dug and finally moved to the other side to dig. They were hoping it wouldn't rain until they were finished. I happened to think mud would be easier to dig but what did I know, I was only a little kid.

When Carter and Mitch were not around I always went to the digging and looked down inside trying to see the other side. It was kind of exciting, at least exciting for a 6 year old. Actually the tunnel was still two holes in the ground. When the tunnel was completed, if it ever was finished, it would probably only be about 8 feet long. Like I said, this was Hog Holler and we didn't have big hills to dig in.

The weather held and finally Carter and Mitch were nearing the end of their work. I have to give them that, they kept at it. Every day I inspected their work and I couldn't see the end of either hole. (It never occurred to me that it was so dark in the holes, that no matter how deep it was, I wouldn't have been able to see the end anyway.)

The big day arrived. Carter and Mitch finished their tunnel. They were so excited they were running around all excited. (You know, it is exciting to start a big project and see it through to an end. If it is successful, they makes it even more exciting.) Carter started yelling for us to come see.

"Mother, Daddy, come see. We finished!" (You notice he didn't call my name. Aren't big brothers wonderful.)

We came running. Carter and Mitch were each standing at one of the ends of the tunnel. We walked over to where Carter was standing.

"I'm going to take the first trip through the tunnel and Mitch will come out here."

Carter got down on his hands and knees and started crawling into the tunnel. Soon he disappeared. A few minutes later we saw his blond head coming out of the tunnel. It was Mitch. He was excited!

"That was great! Don't ya'll want to go through it."

My Daddy just looked at him but my Mother was nice about it.

"Mitch, thank's for the offer but I think we'll probably pass." She smiled at Mitch and she and my daddy went back to whatever they were doing. I stayed behind just hoping.

Like any kid, 6 or otherwise, I wanted to go through the tunnel. I was ignored. I wouldn't ask but I was determined to go through that tunnel.

I watched for a while. Carter and Mitch took turns going back and forth through the tunnel. They might not have cared but being 6 I didn't chance it. I finally wandered back to the house. I had a plan.

I knew that eventually I would be able to go through that tunnel if I was patient long enough. You know, patience is not usually a 6 year old's strongest trait but as a young child I learned that if I wanted something bad enough, all I usually had to do was wait and it would happen.

Carter and Mitch soon got bored with their tunnel and moved on to something else. Have you noticed that a lot of the time the doing is more fun than the actual completion? (That's pretty deep. You'll have to think about that one for a while.)

I picked my time well. Carter and Mitch were gone somewhere and Mother and Daddy were busy doing something away from the tunnel area. I walked up to the tunnel and looked in one side and then the other. Now that the time was here, I was suddenly not so eager to go through with it. It was so dark down there.

I stood there and thought. I had to do it. If I didn't I would wonder my whole life what it was like to crawl through that stupid tunnel. I finally got my courage up and got down on my hands and knees. I started in. It was so dark and because Carter and Mitch can't dig straight the other end was not immediately seen. Remember, I was 6 and a little boy. To me, a short tunnel turned out to be a much longer distance.

I started in and going slowly it was okay. About halfway I stopped. Part of the tunnel had collapsed. Not entirely but enough to scare me. I had to decide to go on or try to back out. If I hadn't stopped I probably would have been all right but now I was stuck in that dark tunnel and I had time to think about where I was and what might happen. (Remember, I told you I had a great imagination.)

I decided to back out. I went in the tunnel. Now I decided to get out. Backing out goes by much slower. I started getting scared and I panicked. I started screaming for my parents. My mother finally heard me and came running. I heard her yelling.

"Riley, where are you?"

"Mama, I'm in here. I can't git out!"

"Riley, why are you in there!" (Now I would probably ask why she was asking me such a dumb question but at the time I just wanted her to help me out.)

"Mama, help me. I'm stuck!"

My mother got down on her hands and knees and looked in the tunnel.

"I see your feet but I can't reach them. You are going to have to back out some so I can reach you."

I thought if I could do that I wouldn't needed her.

"Mama, I can't" I think I was starting to get hysterical.

"Riley, you are just going to have to back out enough so I can grab your feet and pull you out. You can do it."

I started back, slowly I'm sure. With not too much space I soon felt someone grab my feet. I'm sure glad I knew that's what my mother was going to do because that would have scared me even more.

I got out and I was covered in dirt. I found out later that the tunnel had collapsed on that far end and I would never have been able to get through.

I have to give my mother credit. She never fussed at me. She only said one thing to me.

"Riley, the next time you decide to crawl in somewhere. Be sure you can get out on your own. I'm too old to do stuff like this too much. Now, let's go get you cleaned up."

That was all. I don't know if she ever said anything about it to my Daddy or Carter either. I know I never would have heard the end of it if she had told Carter. I did notice later that the tunnel was completely caved in like someone had been trying to turn the tunnel from a tunnel into a ditch. And you know I didn't say anything until now.

Jeff Cavaness

I DON'T LIKE PINK RABBITS

I used to be sick every time we had a holiday from school. I got a lot of ear infections when I was young. This story is about me being sick on a holiday.

The time was nearing Easter. I loved Easter. I love it now because of the significance it means for being a Christian but when I was little I loved it because of the Easter Bunny and hunting eggs and candy.

When I was young my Sunday School Class would always have a party on Easter Sunday afternoon. One year when I was around 10 years old we were having a party at one of the teachers' homes and we were hunting eggs. They would always have a prize egg which meant whoever found the prize egg would receive a prize. I happened to find the prize egg that year and I was so excited when I found it I bumped my head and cut it in the excitement. (The prize was a chocolate bunny. My mother ended up eating it. I just wanted to find it, not eat it. That part would probably be different now.)

Anyway, this particular Easter I had another ear infection. (For all those of you who care, I eventually outgrew the ear infections.) I was about 7 I guess. I had been sick for most of the week leading up to Easter and was still in bed when Easter Sunday came. That meant I would miss out on the Easter party at church and hunting and hiding eggs and playing in general.

Hog Hollow

I guess my mother felt sorry for me and decided to do something extra special for me. Remember, I have told you I liked stuffed animals. But at this point I'm 8 and a stuffed animal would not be at the top of my list for a gift. Don't get me wrong, I liked and still like stuffed animals but I would probably have asked for something if I had had a choice.

My mother decided to surprise me on Easter morning with a 4 foot tall bright pink bunny rabbit. To make it even more special she sneaked into my room and put in on a table at the foot of my bed. On Easter morning I woke up very early for some reason. It was still early enough that the light was very dim in the room. Remember, I am recovering from a high fever from an ear infection.

I am barely awake and I look around and see that big, ol' rabbit staring at me and I start screaming. Of course that wakes up the entire house and my mother comes running. By that time I am fully awake and realize what the rabbit truly is but I'm upset. My mother comes in and calms me down and tells me she bought the rabbit for me. I thanked her but you know, I never much liked that rabbit. It was one of my stuffed animals that didn't get much bed time.

LISTEN TO THE BIRDS

Have you ever been outside and just listened to the birds? Well, I have. Of course, there has been some mornings that I wished those birds would shut up so I could sleep, but all in all, they are pretty neat to have around. This story is about how "listening to the birds" may have saved my life.

As I have told you I liked to roam the pastures

and woods. Behind our house, way back over the hill, was this small natural valley with this spring-fed pond. It was a great place to play. It was hidden from our house but actually not that far away.

I would play frontiersman and Indians and horses. The game of horses either consisted of me pretending I was a horse or me riding my stick horse. Did you ever ride a stick horse? That was fun. You know, we had horses, real horses, but I think my stick horse was more fun. It definitely would do what I wanted it to do without balking. My stick horse's name was Beauty. I think I had just read <u>Black Beauty</u> and that's how I came up with my horse's name. Actually, the games I played were usually about something I was reading or had read. I loved to read and still do. Books make excellent places to get ideas for playing.

Anyway, you know how I feel about snakes and being a farm, we had lots of snakes. The problem was that not all of them were harmless.

Because of that I was careful of where I played

and especially what time of the year I played in the pastures and the woods.

One early spring day I went back to the valley to play. The sun was out but I believed it was still too early and cold for snakes to be out and around. (Can you see where this story is going?) I hadn't been there too long and I was on the bank of the pond playing. Actually, I don't remember just what I was playing but I'm sure it was important at the time.

I was playing and suddenly I noticed that there were no birds singing.

That was strange because they were always singing, especially in the woods.

I looked around and couldn't see any cause for no birds singing. I don't know why but something compelled me to look behind me and down on the ground. I almost fainted. There crawling toward me was snake, a water moccasin. If you don't know, water moccasins are extremely poisonous and some consider them more dangerous than rattlesnakes.

Jeff Cavaness

I was literally frozen for a second and then I took off running as fast as I could. I didn't look back or stop until I hit our back porch. I don't know if the snake followed me or not. I kind of doubt it. It was probably only trying to get to the water where it was warmer but I didn't hang around to find out. I got myself to safety. You know, it was a long time before I went back to my valley to play or anything else.

THE COCKER SPANIEL

Living on a farm had its advantages. All kids like animals, well most of them. I was no exception. I loved the animals. Now, don't get me wrong; sometimes I hated having to take of 'em but all in all, I like having them around. I believe that every child should have a dog some time or another if they want one. That's why today my son has two dogs. We're still working on him learning how to take care of 'em. I have already had that pleasure. I also believe that every child should learn to take care of their pets, dogs or otherwise.

Anyway, we had dogs. We had coonhound dogs. They were hunting dogs. My daddy raised and trained them for sale. Sometimes we would have the puppies sold before they were even born. Apparently, my daddy was a good trainer of dogs. But on my level as a little boy, I just wanted a puppy to love and play with. I soon learned to not get too attached to any of the dogs. About the time I was used to having it around, my daddy would sell it. One time I had a dog named Lucy. She had been born on my birthday. I loved Lucy. I was able to keep her for a couple of years. That was the longest time I had ever been able to keep one. One summer I went on a trip with some cousins and when I got back Lucy was gone. My daddy had sold her. I never got attached to another dog.

Back to my original story, one day a beautiful golden cocker spaniel showed up on our doorstep.

She was friendly and seemed glad to be there. I begged my parents to let me keep her. My daddy was not too enthusiastic about it but he let me keep her. I named her Blonde. (I know, not too original.) We fed her and fixed a place for her to sleep. I played with her and had the greatest time. She was mine. She wasn't a hound dog that someone else might want.

She was all mine. Three days later she disappeared. We hunted and hunted.

Of course, I thought something had happened to her or the hounds had killed her or something else equally horrible.

We never did see hide nor hair of her again. I finally decided she had been just traveling through. She had found a nice, safe place to stay and rest up with plenty of food. I hope to think she had a good time with me too but I'll never know. I just hope whoever she was traveling toward knows what a great dog she was.

Jeff Cavaness

THE WILLOW TREE

Do you know what a willow tree looks like? They are sometimes called weeping willow trees. It is green with long skinny branches that droop down and hide the trunk of the tree. When a willow tree gets full grown you can push your way through the branches and close to the tree trunk you will find a hidden world. At least, when you're a little boy, you think it's a hidden world.

Jeff Cavaness

Me thinking that is the reason for this story.

We didn't have any weeping willow trees on our farm but Uncle Linus and Aunt Rosie did. Now Uncle Linus and Aunt Rosie were probably the richest of my kin. They had a farm four times larger than ours and had a lot more farm machinery too. They raised hogs but not on as big a scale as we did. I don't know why they was richer except maybe it was because Uncle Linus and Aunt Rosie didn't have any kids. They had had one who died when he was a baby and then there were no more to come. I always thought the reason my Uncle Linus had such a big place was because he needed something to keep his mind off not having any children. I used to visit my cousin's grave sometimes. It was in the Standfield Chapel Presbyterian Church graveyard. My Aunt Rosie was great to be around. Iliked my Uncle Linus but he was abrupt and didn't have a lot of time for a little boy. Now, it was always okay with him for me to come stay with them but it was Aunt Rosie that paid me the most attention. She was forever cooking for me and giving me little stuff. Plus, they lived in this gigantic old farmhouse that had an upstairs and an attic. It was a great house to play in.

Anyway, the willow tree was in their front yard close to the road.

When I was a little boy I used to play in the yard and especially under that willow tree. One day in particular I was up under there playing and got hot.

One thing you need to know about weeping willow trees, it gets hot under all those swaying, weeping branches. To look at it though, you would think it would be cool under there, it ain't.

Some of the men that Uncle Linus hired to work on his place (I told you he was rich.) was nearby working on some machinery. I could hear them but I didn't believe they knew I was there because they had come after I had gotten under there. I was wrong.

Because I had gotten so hot I came up with a great idea. I decided I would take off all my clothes. I decided no one could see me and it would be kinda fun and dangerous to be outside with all my clothes off and even though those men were so close. I believed those men couldn't see me and it would be my little joke. (Do I need to tell you? The joke ended up being on me.)

I took my clothes off and paraded around under that weeping willow tree. I played and thought I was so smart for pulling such a big joke on everyone. I finally put my clothes on and played some more and by then the men had gone off somewhere. I left the willow tree and went back into the house. I forgot all about it until it slapped me in the face that night at the supper table.

I was sitting there with Uncle Linus and Aunt Rosie eating one of Aunt Rosie's great meals.

"Rosie, do you know what my men told me this afternoon?"

I was busy eating. I was only halfway listening. My Aunt Rosie was a great cook and I was giving it my full attention. When I came to visit Aunt Rosie usually cooked all my favorites so I was enjoying the meal.

"What did they say?"

"They said that this afternoon they saw the strangest bird out under the willow tree."

Uncle Linus had my attention now.

"They said it was a funny color and moved around like it was in pain."

"What was it?"

"I don't know. They said it was so strange looking they decided to leave it alone and hope it would go away. Riley, do you know anything about it? You were out playing out there this afternoon, weren't you?"

"Yeah, Uncle Linus, but I don't remember seeing any strange bird."

I was sweating bullets by now. I was so embarrassed. What was going on? Did those men see a strange bird or did they see me?

"Well, Riley, maybe you ought not to play around that tree for a while. We can't be sure what they saw. I don't want you getting into trouble. I can't have my men scared off by some strange looking bird, now can I?"

Uncle Linus looked at me and smiled. I guess I kinda smiled back. I just knew I wanted them to talk about something else.

I don't think I went near that tree for ages after that. One thing I learned and I'm passing it on to you. Just because you think you're hidden by the weeping willow tree's branches, you ain't!

BREEDING CATTLE AIN'T GOOD SUPPER TABLE TALK

If you know anything about working farms, especially ones with animals, you know that keeping everything bred is a high priority. (For all you city people, bred means pregnant or expecting.) So births and animals being "in heat" was topic that discussed quite regularly even at the supper table.

With that thought in mind let me tell you about a certain time when we had a family over for supper and I got into big trouble because I tried to discuss animals being bred and such.

On that fateful (Isn't fateful a great word.) afternoon I and my daddy were down at my granddaddy's. I don't know if'n I ever told you about my granddaddy. I loved my granddaddy. He always had a kind word for me and was always sneaking quarters to me when my grandmamma wasn't watching.

He'd say, "Now Riley, just keep this a secret between the two of us, okay. There ain't no sense of letting on to your grandmamma what I done. Okay!"

"Sure, Granddaddy. I won't tell nobody."

I miss him still today. He died my senior year in college. He was a good man. I like to sing at church. I believe I inherited that from him. I would sit next to him in church, my grandmamma played the piano for the choir, and listen to him sing. I didn't know it at time but my granddaddy had the most beautiful tenor voice. I knew then I just liked to listen to him sing.

Anyway, my grandparents lived just down the road from us. Granddaddy owned a bull. We never both had a bull at the same time. Bulls aren't the most friendly animals on any level and they sure ain't friendly to each other so my daddy and granddaddy just kept one for both farms.

That afternoon my daddy and I had taken three heifers, young female cows, down my granddaddy's to put with the bull to be bred. If you don't know nothing about farm animals young heifers have a tendency to be skittish (Skittish – that's fun word to say.) around bulls. At the time I thought they looked like they were flirting but I don't think that was it. Now, I've watched animals breeding lots of times so what was happening was not particularly interesting until one of the heifers flat refused to let the bull do his stuff. This got my attention because my daddy and granddaddy seemed concerning about what was not happening. I started watching the bull and the heifer closer and actually I thought it looked quite comical. (Do you know what comical means?

It means funny.) The way that bull and heifer was going around each other and that heifer trying her best to get away from that bull. I finally had to laugh.

"Riley." My daddy didn't think it was comical or funny.

I tried after that to not laugh out loud but it was hard. I felt like I was watching some television program. (I bet you thought life on the farm was dull.)

After what seemed an awful long time of waiting and watching, my daddy and granddaddy decided to give up on the third heifer. They got the bull out and put back in his pasture and then Daddy and I took our three heifers back to our pasture. My daddy was not happy about the total outcome of the afternoon. (I told you. Making sure every animal is pregnant is important business on the farm.)

Now, we come to the climax of the story.

(Climax is a new word for me.

It means I'm going to explain the title of this tale.) That night we had our closest neighbors, besides my grandparents, to supper. They lived maybe one half mile away from us. They had a daughter that was about three years younger than me. Her name was Polly. We would play together occasionally when our mothers got together but there wasn't much we could play because she was a girl and so much younger. But I liked her and she was fun sometimes.

We were sitting around the kitchen table eating and I was listening to the grownups talking. Now, if you ain't noticed, I like to talk. And not being able to talk when adults was talking was very hard on me. As they were talking the conversation turned to them talking about someone at church being reluctant to do something or other. I don't remember the specifics, just that they were talking about someone having to be prodded, you know – encouraged, to do something. I was sitting there thinking about what I could add to the conversation. I couldn't help myself. I wanted to be part of the conversation.

As I listened to the grownups talk a brilliant idea came to my head.

"I know what ya'll are talking about. It's just like those heifers this afternoon when we were trying to get to go to the bull. One of those heifers just wouldn't go to that bull. I thought it was funny but Daddy and Granddaddy didn't. We just couldn't understand why that heifer wouldn't go to the bull."

The room had gotten real quiet. I stopped talking and looked around.

Miss Esther, Polly's mother, was looking all embarrassed and my daddy was frowning at me and Polly and her daddy just kept on eating. I didn't understand why everyone had quit talking. I looked at my mother.

"Riley, that is not proper talk for the supper table."

"Mama, what do you mean?" I couldn't understand what she was saying.

We talked about animals 'most every night. Why should tonight be any different.

"Riley, cattle breeding is not a good subject for conversation at the supper table." She looked at me real stern-like and changed the subject. I guess I got all embarrassed and got to thinking was I in trouble and what would happen to me after our company left.

Actually, nothing happened to me. I never brought it up and neither did either of my parents. I will tell you something though. I never brought up cattle breeding or any other kind of breeding at the supper table ever.

Jeff Cavaness

MISS CONNIE AND THE FISH

There was an older lady that lived in Standfield Chapel by the name of Miss Connie. I'm sure she had more of a name than that but Miss Connie was all I ever knew. Now, if Miss Connie was kin to the Standfields', I didn't know it but she was close to the family anyhow. Well, one day Miss Connie gave my daddy a cat. She was white with a gray patch on her forehead. My daddy came up with the name, Miss Connie, for the cat. (That was original, wasn't it.) Miss Connie, the cat, is who this story is about.

Miss Connie lived on our place for many years. I believe, before she died, she had several generations of her offspring around her. (Offspring, doesn't look anything like what it means, does it.) I named her kittens and could tell them apart usually. You know, I never knew who the kittens' father was ever.

Miss Connie was a great cat. I loved playing with her and talking to her.

She would bring her newest batch of kittens to me and I would pet them and talk to them. I guess she trusted me and knew I would never hurt them. As I got older I started noticing that while we always fed the dogs and the rest of the animals, we never set out any food for Miss Connie or her kittens. I finally asked my mother why this was and she told me they wouldn't feed the cats because they wanted them to hunt the mice and rats that lived in the barns. The mice and rats would eat

Hog Hollow

the corn and other pig food we had stored in the barns so we needed Miss Connie and her family to help keep the mice and rat populations down. (Let me tell you a secret. I understood what my mother was saying but I still snuck food to Miss Connie's kittens every chance I got.)

Well, because of not being fed on a regular basis Miss Connie had to hunt and taught her children how to hunt mice and rats. One day I was out playing in one of the back pastures when I saw Miss Connie walking away from the barn. I guess I was bored or intrigued (What a great word!) and I followed her to see where she was going and what she was going to do. I followed her to one of our ponds in one of the cow pastures. Now you and I both know that cats don't like the water too much so I wondered what she was going to do. I knew she could get water to drink closer to the house and barns so what was she doing out there by the pond. She stopped by the edge of the water and just looked in the water. At least, that's what I thought she was doing. I watched for a while and then I got bored with watching her because she was sitting so still and doing nothing. As I walked back to the house it hit me! Miss Connie was fishing. I know it sounded funny for a cat to be fishing but what else why would she be doing there staring in the water for so long. When I got to the house I ran into the house to find my mother.

"Mama, do you know what I just found out?"

"No, what Riley?"

"You will never believe this. Miss Connie is fishing up at the pond behind the barn."

"Riley, you know cats don't like the water. What makes you think she's fishing?"

"Because she has been sitting there for so long and just staring at the water and doing nothing."

"Riley, I don't know what she's doing but I don't think Miss Connie is fishing. Cats do not like water."

"Mama, I know what I saw."

I ran out not understanding why my mother didn't believe me but I went and told my daddy and my brother and they both laughed at me. I stopped talking about it then.

Then a few days later we happened to all be out in the back yard when here come Miss Connie pulling a big ole catfish that was almost as big as she was. My mother, brother and daddy all looked at Miss Connie and then at each other and then they turned and looked at me. I just smiled and turned around and went in the house.

Jeff Cavaness

REGGIE AND THE MAMA PIG

I remember one summer day when my cousin Reggie came over to play.

Now you need to know something about Reggie before I go on. Reggie was a city kid. Where he lived there was upwards to ten thousand people. Plus, another important fact; Reggie was from the other side of the family, my mother's side. According to the Standfields', my mother's side of the family didn't know nothing about farming and especially about hogs.

I guess I need to explain why knowing about hogs is so important. When you live with hogs and depend on them for your livelihood, (That's another good word, I wonder where I heard that one.) you need to know all about 'em.

Now we had hogs. I mean lots of hogs; hundreds of hogs. Sometimes when I was trying to help feed and water 'em I thought we had thousands. (Now I ain't never seen thousands of pigs together but I can imagine, can't I.) If you have never been around hogs when they are hungry, I can tell you, they ain't patient animals. But to us, hogs were our source of food and money to pay our bills.

We raised hogs to feed ourselves and to feed others. When the hogs reached a certain weight, we took 'em to the hog barn in town to sell to the slaughterhouse, which in turn used hogs to make sausage, ham, and bacon.

(Hey, you didn't think that all that meat you

been eating just came from the store wrapped up in those packages, did you?"). Well, because of all this, taking care of hogs was very important to us and all of our kin. If you didn't understand that fact, you just didn't understand us.

Another thing you ought to know about Reggie is that he was a troublemaker. I don't mean he was bad so much as he was always getting into something he wasn't 'posed to and dragging my along with 'im. I guess I should of known better but even if'n I had known, I probably would of done it anyway if I thought it would've been fun. When Reggie came to spend the day we would light out over the fields to see what we could see. That's one thing about growing up surrounded by kin, you can go anywhere you want and not have to worry about being somewhere you ain't 'posed to be.

After Reggie and me had sufficiently looked around to see what we could git into we drifted back to the house and ran in the back door asking my mother for something to eat. (You know, boys are always hungry,) Reggie loved mayonnaise sandwiches and I liked butter sandwiches. We set out on the back porch eating our sandwiches and drinking milk. From our back porch you could see four of our pig lots. We kept different age pigs in different lots. In the lot closest to us was a mama sow and her baby pigs. One thing about hogs, when they are babies they are the cutest things. Anyway, Reggie got up and walked over to the fence and looked at the baby pigs.

"Riley, you think we could play with those little pigs?"

If you don't know hogs you need to know that mama sows don't like nobody messing with their babies. In face, not any hog on the place likes anybody messing with any pig, baby or otherwise. To prove this whenever a pig or hog squeals every hog on the place starts squealing and running and carrying on like nothing you ain't never heard before. If'n we ever had to work on a pig we had to make sure none of the other hogs could get to us because they would eat us up.

Hog Hollow

I mentioned this fact to Reggie but he didn't seem to hear because before I could stop him he hopped over the fence and started walking toward the baby pigs. I have to admit baby pigs are cute. There's no doubt about it, but they ain't too easy to play with when their mamas is around. Anyway, Reggie slowly crept up behind one of the baby pigs and grabbed it. I could have told him that's not a real smart thing to do. Well, that baby pig started squealing and carrying on like it was being hurt. It wasn't but let somebody grab you from behind and lift you way up in the air and see if you don't start squealing too.

When that baby pig started squealing all the other pigs started squealing and then the mama sow got into the act. She whirled around from what she was eating. (Hogs are always eating), and started for Reggie. She was not happy. I yelled for Reggie to put the pig down and git out of there, but he ignored me. (I was beginning to think Reggie wasn't the smartest cousin I had. Well, he is from the other side of the family.) I kept yelling at Reggie until he finally saw the sow coming towards him. Let me tell you, when you see a big ol' sow charging toward you; you need to drop anything you're holding and start running. Of course, bright Reggie ran in the wrong direction. I yelled for Reggie to run for the lot gate. He ignored me. He ran for a cow trough. (We kept a few cows too.) The sow was about as tall as the cow trough. Reggie ran and jumped up in the trough. He was grinning. I'm sure he thought he had outsmarted the sow. He was wrong. That old sow ran right smack into that trough and knocked it over. That sent Reggie flying. When he finally stopped rolling, he had stopped grinning. The best thing about what the sow had done was now Reggie was close to the fence and he got up and ran and climbed over.

I was the one doing the grinning now.

Because of all the shouting and screaming, Reggie's mother and mine had come out to see what was going on. I quickly told 'em nothing was going on and that they could just go on back inside 'cause we was having fun. My mother kind of shot me a warning look but she and my aunt left us alone. I actually don't know if Reggie would have gotten in trouble but I wasn't willing to take any chances on him or me gittin' in hot water. "Cause I know if'n Reggie had of gotten in trouble somehow I would have too.

You know though, Reggie never did have anything else to do with hogs, baby or otherwise.

Jeff Cavaness

PARTY LINE

I don't remember when we didn't have a telephone but I do remember us having a party line. For all those who don't know what a party line is, it is when more than one family share the same line. Each family would have a different ring that would let them know the call coming through was for them. Ours was 3 short rings.

The best thing about party lines was that you

could pick up and listen to others talk. You know, if I wanted to just pick up the phone and see what was happening, I might hear most anyone talking about who knows what.

Remember, I'm about 4 or 5 and I really probably don't understand what I'm doing or at least that's my story and I'm sticking to it.

One day I was bored and no one was around to tell me not to. I picked up the phone and heard two women talking. I didn't recognize their voices but remember I was little. They was gossiping about some other lady. I listened until I got bored with that. (I'm sure that didn't take long.)

The next day I did the same thing. Those two same women were on the phone talking about someone else. Now, this conversation was not very nice about the person they were talking about. I listened again until I got bored and then went off to play. The next day I did the same thing. I picked up the phone and heard those two same ladies talking about someone else. This time I recognized who they were talking about. It was a

Hog Hollow

lady from our church. This time I didn't get bored. I listened until I made the mistake of breathing too loud into the phone.

One of the women said, "Did you hear something? Do you think someone is listening?"

The other lady said, "I think so. I just don't understand why some people have to be so rude as to listen to other people's conversations." (I wanted to ask if it was rude to talk bad about someone on the phone too. But I didn't.)

I still didn't say anything. I was afraid to move or even breathe. Idon't know if they knew who I was or what. They went on talking about people listening and I finally got bored and hung up the phone.

I didn't try to listen for a couple of days. One day I picked up and the ladies were at it again. I must've not done a good job of being quiet because I heard one of the women say, "Did you hear that? They're back to listening again."

It shocked me so bad I hung up the phone quickly. The next day was Sunday and when we got to church I saw the lady I had heard the other two women talking about. I wondered if I should tell her what I had heard. I thought about it. I decided against it. I decided if I told her everyone would know I had been listening on the party line.

You know, I still wonder if that was the right decision. I did listen occasionally after that and I never heard those two ladies talking about that lady again. I guess I made the right decision.

THE GRAVEYARD

Remember I told you about our church, Standfield Chapel Presbyterian Church. Well, it had a great graveyard. It was perched up on a hill and some would probably call it peaceful. It was about a mile's walk from my house and every once in a while I would go up there and have a look around and play.

What I liked about it was that it is full of big old

tombstones. The graveyard itself was about two hundred years old. You could walk through there and see names and dates that went way back. It was kind of fun to walk through and read my family names and see how many people I been kin to and who had died. Don't tell anybody and especially don't tell my parents or teachers, it was fun to look at the dates and figure how old some of the those people were when they died. It was always kind of sad when I figured how that person on the tombstone had been a little kid when he or she had died. It sometimes made me think what kind of life they had had all those years ago. I wondered sometimes if they used to run and play in this same graveyard just like I like to do. Anyway, it was something to think about.

My friends and I used to run and hide behind those old tombstones jumping out trying to scare each other. At Vacation Bible School the highlight was the free time we had and we would run to the graveyard and play. Of course, once in a while one of the old people at the church would get a

Hog Hollow

bee in their bonnet about how disrespectful it was when we played in the graveyard.

Then we would have to quit for a while. But it wouldn't be long before they would start grumbling about something else and we would be out there running and jumping again.

There was one time we should have listened to all of the old folks. One night in particular we were running and yelling and having a great time. When it was time to leave we were yelling for each other to come on and go back inside the church. My cousin, Reggie, was visiting so he could attend Bible School was with us. Reggie didn't answer or come. The rest of us just thought he was playing a trick on us and laughed at him and went on back inside. It was just like Reggie to try to scare us or even worse, get us all in trouble. What did he care, this wasn't his church. When he didn't come to class and the teachers started asking about him, we got worried. Reggie was capable of playing many a joke but this was going on a little long even for him. Finally we told the teachers what was going on and we didn't know what was going on.

The teachers told our parents and we all went back out in the graveyard to look for our Reggie. What us kids didn't know was that the next day there was to be a funeral at the church and the gravediggers had been there that same day to ready the grave for the burial. We hunted all over and narrowed it down to the far side of the graveyard. Of course, the far side of the graveyard was also where it was the darkest at night. With our flashlights, we slowly looked everywhere for Reggie. Someone yelled and we looked and saw an open grave.

I went over and looked in. Reggie was in the bottom knocked out cold. He must have been running and not seen the opening and fell in. Unconscious he couldn't hear us calling for him. A couple of the men jumped in and pulled Reggie out. He was okay and just a little scared. You know, he didn't try to pull anymore tricks during that Vacation Bible School.

FRONTIER CAMPFIRE

Remember me telling you about my little valley back in the fields behind my house. When I was about 10 or 11 I was back there playing like I was a explorer/settler in the New World. I decided I needed a fire to make it even more authentic. (Authentic – that is a great word. It sounds like it should mean more than, real.)

I approached my father with that idea.

"Would it be okay if I built a campfire back there in the field? Iwould make sure there wasn't anything that could catch on fire. I would put rocks around the fire and I'd be real careful. Please."

"Riley, you know how dangerous fires are. I don't think you ought to do that. I know you'll be careful but I don't think you need to be doing that. Okay."

I looked at him real pitiful like. It didn't work. "Okay."

I was so disappointed. I wanted that fire. By now I had worked myself up so much about having a fire that I believed having a fire was the only way I could have a good time playing.

Being a typical kid I decided that my father was just being too careful and I could have a fire and not get into trouble. I got some matches and put them in my coat pocket when no one was watching. I picked a good day and off to my valley I went. When I got there I cleared a place and got some rocks and made a ring. Then I got a great idea. I would burn dry grass. I decided dry grass would burn quick and I could actually burn more of it.

I gathered the grass and made a pile. I stuck a match and the grass started burning instantly. One thing I didn't plan on; dry grass may burn quickly but it also produces a lot of smoke. When I saw how much smoke was happening I hurriedly stomped the fire out and even put water on what was left of my fire. (I was close to a pond.) I was so disappointed but not enough to get myself in big trouble with my father. I can't imagine what would happen to me if he knew I had started a fire anyway. (Especially when he told me not to.)

I guess I should say when my father found out. I assumed everyone in the whole county saw all that smoke and I imagined my father hollering for me at any minute.

You know, he never did. Fact is, not one word was ever said about my fire. If my father ever knew about it, he didn't say anything and you know I didn't say anything.

I learned a lesson that day. I supposed I should

have learned the lesson of obeying my parents or something like that. What I learned was that I needed to be sure of what I was burning before setting fire to it.

THE TRUTH COMES OUT

My mother is great. She was strict but she loved me and for the most part, she was an encourager. Remember, I turned from farming and wanted to go to college and teach and do theatre and write. She didn't have anyone in her or my father's family to compare me to. I was different.

In most kids' lives there comes a time when

they find out about their parents. They find out that their parents were just like them. Their parents were kids who played and occasionally got in trouble for something. I remember the day distinctly (another good word) when I found out the truth about my mother.

When my mother was a little girl she went to a small community school. She told me she went to a school that most of the kids were all in the same room with the one teacher. I couldn't hardly imagine that then and now after being a teacher, I really can't imagine how hard that must have been for the teacher and students.

My mother said she loved school. She loved to read and that part was true. She was always reading and she still reads a lot. She read to me from back when I can remember and now reads to my son. She says she was a good student and generally liked going to school. There was one aspect of her childhood she left out until this particular day.

My mother apparently was a little troublemaker.

She finally came out with the following story.

"Riley, I'm telling you this story because I want you to know that everyone gets into trouble sometime or another. The secret is what do you do after the trouble."

I was interested. I just knew this was going to be a great story.

My mother continued.

"There was another little girl in the school that I didn't much like. I really can't remember exactly why I didn't like her but the important part of this story is that we didn't get along. One day I and the other little girl had gotten into an argument over something."

"What over?"

"I don't know. I have forgotten by now. That was a long time ago."

(I have always doubted that fact.) I was angry and started looking for some way to get at the other girl. Now, remember this school was in the deep south. On hot days there was not air conditioning and maybe now even fans except the ones the kids made from pieces of paper. On hot days sometimes some of the kids would go down to a creek that had water in it and swim.

Now, for the kids to do this we had to take all of our clothes off so we would have something to put on to go back to class. We would do this during our lunch break. Remember, this was before cafeterias and fast food places."

"On the day of the argument the other little girl and some of her friends decided to go down to the creek and play in the water. I saw them go. I decided to follow them and see what they were up to. I followed along and discovered what they were doing; they were going to the creek. I waited to give them time to get their clothes off and get in the water. I crept up and took her clothes. I started back to the schoolhouse when I heard her start screaming and this brought the teacher and the girl immediately accused my mother of stealing her clothes. (I always wanted to know if she was naked while she was screaming and accusing my mother.) The teacher came to find me and asked me about what had happened. I confessed to the whole deed." (My mother may have played a mean joke on her enemy but she was not a liar about it. She didn't hesitate to speak up and take credit for it.)

"The teacher punished her and so did my father. I forget what happened at school but she got a whipping with a strap at home. I never did anything like that again. (I still wonder if that's true.)

Jeff Cavaness

REGGIE AND OLD MAN PALMER

I've talked a lot about Reggie, let me tell you what finally taught Reggie to listen to me when I say something.

It was one hot summer afternoon and we were at the graveyard running around playing. (This was before Reggie fell in the grave.) We were having a good time playing follow the leader and such when Reggie yelled, "Look!"

I looked up, "What?"

"There," he said, "what's down that road?"

Reggie was pointing towards a little road that led around the back of the graveyard and into the woods. I looked at Reggie and looked back at the woods.

"Come on, Reggie, let's keep playing. There's nothing down there. It's just a road."

Reggie started walking toward the woods.

"Where you going now?" I yelled at him.

"Come on, Riley, let's see what's down there."

I didn't want to. I knew what was down that road. I just couldn' t figure out how to convince Reggie he didn't need to know.

"Reggie, don't go. We're have fun doing this. It's just some dumb ol' dirt road. Why do you want to go in the woods?"

He kept going.

"Come on, Riley. It'll be fun. It's hot out here. It'll be cooler under them trees. Come on with me. I'll race you."

With that he took off running. It had to go. I had to catch him before he got us both in trouble we might not git out of. What Reggie didn't know as that there was somethin' down that road. It was somethin' that every kid in our community knew about and every parent had warned their kids about. Down the road was a house and in that house live Ol' Man Palmer. He was the meanest man I'd ever seen. He was the meanest man anybody ever seen. I don't mean he wouldn't speak to you or he wouldn't wave at you as you passed by; he was nasty mean. He went out of his way to be mean. It was said that if'n anybody's cat or dog showed up missing, you could probably find it at Mr.

Palmer's if'n you was brave enuf to go look. "Coursen your dog or cat would probably be dead or worse. I myself had seen him picking up dead possums and coons on the side of the road. And I don't think it was because he wanted to clean up the road either.

Reggie was determined to go see what he could see down the road.

Now, I will say that on a hot summer afternoon that cool dirt road look inviting.

The road was shaded by the trees and you could feel a breeze coming through the leaves. The problem was that that road led to Ol' Man Palmer's old house.

A couple of years before me and some of the other kids at church had wanted to do the same thing Reggie wanted to do, explore that road and them woods.

Nobody could tell us nothing so off we went. Actually, nothing happened except Ol' Man Palmer coming out of his house and yelling at us to git off his property. I don't know if'n it was his property but we go and we got good.

Since then I never had the desire to go down that road again. Now, here was Reggie wanting to do the same thing.

I finally caught up to Reggie and grabbed him.

"Hey, will ya wait a minute."

"Riley, what's your problem? I just want to see what's down this road. Come on, it might be fun."

"Reggie, I know what's down that road and I've been down it and I don't want to go down it agin."

"Riley, come on, are you scared?"

"You mighty right, I'm scared and you would be too if you knew what I knew."

"Okay, what do you know? Why shouldn't I want to go down that road?"

"Because at the end of that road if Ol' Man Palmer's house and he don't like no visitors!"

"We ain't gonna hurt nothing at that old man's house. Come on, Riley. Let's go on down there. It'll be fun."

We stood there at the edge of the woods for a while arguing. Reggie knew me too well. He knew if he begged long enif I would go along with him. He could see I was weakening.

"Come on, Riley, let's go."

He started down the road. I reluctantly followed. I kept asking myself just how did I let myself get into these things.

The only good thin about going down that road was that it was cool. We had both gotten hot running around in the graveyard. But I can tell you just gitting cooled off was not a good enuf reason for being on that road in those woods. We walked a little ways until we saw the top of Ol' Man Palmer's house. When we did I grabbed Reggie and made him listen to all I knew about Ol' Man Palmer and tried agin to convince him to turn around and leave before it was too late. Guess what, Reggie just laughed at me.

When we came into view of the front of the house we stopped. There was no sign of life. That in itself was strange in Standfield Chapel. There wasn't no family that didn't have at least one ol' hound dog laying around.. But Ol' Man Palmer didn't have no animals around, not even hogs. (That should tell you something right there. What kind of person doesn't keep hogs in Hog Holler?)

We walked a little closer. Still no sign of

nothing.

"Come in, Reggie, you've seen it. Let's go!" I was trying to drag Reggie away.

"Riley, let go. I want to see what's around back. Let's see if we can see any dead animals."

I regretted telling Reggie anything. Did I not tell you he was always getting me in trouble? Here we go agin.

We slowly walked towards the back of the house. I noticed it was awfully quiet. There were no birds or bugs stirring or making any kind of noises. That was strange to be in he middle of the woods. I was gitting scareder and scareder. Reggie didn't seemed to be fazed at all. (Fazed, I like that word.) As we got around the back of the house I heard something crack. Both of us jumped. One good thing, I believed Reggie was finally deciding to be scared too. He would never admit it though. We looked around at each other and then looked around us and at the house. We didn't see anything. At the back of the house was an ol' car with its front wheels up on blocks. I knew that ol' car. It was Ol' Man Palmer's.

"Reggie, come on, let's git out of here. That's his ol' car. He's at home.

He's around here somewheres. Let's go!"

"Riley, has anything happened to us yet? Stop whining. I want to see what's back here."

"Reggie, who cares what's back here. Let's git while the gitting is good!"

"You go if you want to but I'm staying."

I decided I couldn't go home without Reggie. If he got kilt, I might as well git kilt too because I shure couldn't go home without him. Even if'n he had gotten himself kilt, somehow it would've been blamed on me. I might as well stay with him but I didn't like it. I decided if'n we got out of this alive I was gonna tell my Mother to not let Reggie come over to our house anymore. I just couldn't take it.

Reggie had gotten ahead of me. I had decided to just stop and wait.

Maybe he would see something, I don't know what, and decide he had seen enuf and we could go home. Reggie got closer and closer to Ol' Man Palmer's back porch. Any minute I expected to see the back door bust open and Ol' Man Palmer come through it. Not one thing happened. Reggie got all the way to the back porch and even stepped up on it. I almost died then and there when he did that. Reggie jumped off the porch and went over to the ol' car and looked inside. There was a ol' falling down shed out back. Reggie even went over to it and stuck in his head. I half expected him to come out headless. Reggie looked over at me and laughed. He ran over and punched me in the shoulder.

"What a crybaby you are! I told you there wasn't anything to be scared of. I can't wait to tell everybody about this. I can't wait to tell everybody how scared you was." He started back down the road just a giggling. I wished I had somethin' to hit him with. What happened to Ol' Man Palmer? Was what I had heard about him all these years just been a story, a fairy tale?

Reggie practically skipped down the road. He

was so happy. He had shown me up. He kept looking back at me and pointing and laughing. I was looking down kind of dragging my feet. I would glance up at Reggie every once in a while. I was wishing he would trip and fall. I was thinking hard of what I could do to him if he did make fun of me in front of everybody. Just as we go to the end of the road I heard somethin'. I looked up. Reggie had stopped dead in his tracks. Ol' Man Palmer was standing in the middle of the road staring at Reggie. He was holding a shotgun. He just stood there and looked at Reggie. I caught up with Reggie. For some reason, I wasn't scared.

Maybe it was 'cause Ol' Man Palmer wasn't looking at me, he was staring hard at Reggie.

"Boy, did you find anything interesting at my house? I heard your friend here try to git you to leave but you wouldn't listen, would you? That wasn't too smart.

He lifted his shotgun and as he did Reggie took off screaming leaving me there looking at Ol' Man Palmer. Reggie never looked back. Ol"

Man Palmer put the gun down and looked at me and just grinned. At least, I think he grinned. He turned and walked back in the woods. I was dumbfounded.

(That's another great word.)

I finally caught up to Reggie halfway way to my house. He was shaking so bad. I didn't say anything. You know, he never did 'cause me any trouble no more. Maybe Ol'Man Palmer ain't so bad after all. I told you Hog Holler was great place to live.

Jeff Cavaness

THE FIRE AND THE CHICKENS

I have told you a little about my mother but I want to tell you a story that I have always felt so sorry for my mother about.

My mother's family was sharecroppers. For you city folks sharecroppers refers to families that lived on other people's farms and worked the land for them. For this they usually got a house and part of the money for the crops they helped bring in. My mother remembers moving several times during her childhood. The worst part of being a sharecropper was that a lot of people looked down on them for their way of life. Do you remember me telling you that the Standfields' looked down on my mother's family? Well, that was the reason why. The Standfields' owned all their land.

My mother was the 8th child out of 14. I remember telling her she married my father to just get out of the crowd. They never could afford much with all those mouths to feed and because they never stayed any particular place very long, they didn't get to put down roots and settle in with their neighbors or the community. To this day I think this is the reason my mother and her sisters and cousins are so close.

Having a pet was something my mother never really had. She told me once in a while they would have some old dog or a cat that the last renter of the house had left would be around for them to play with but usually pets was something they couldn't afford to have and feed.

One early spring my mother went to her father and begged him to let her get some little chickens to raise. She had discovered through school that the 4-H Club would help her get the chickens and she could raise them and do a project with them. She then would be allowed to keep them for whatever purpose the family had for them. (I'm thinking the purpose would probably be eating but what do I know. I didn't have 13 brothers and sisters.)

The only catch was my mother's family would have to pay to feed and take care of them. Finally, my grandfather relented and they went to get the little chicks. There were 50 of them. My mother was so excited she said.

They were so cute and soft. (You know, little chicks are cute and soft but can you imagine 50 of them at the same time. Can you imagine the noise of all of them cheeping at the same time? How about the mess they would make?) (I wonder if they were as bad as a bunch of pigs.)

Jeff Cavaness

    My mother says they had only had them for a few days when a real cold snap happened. They had been staying chicken coop that some of mother's brothers had built for her. The weather turned off cold like it can do in the spring. My mother was afraid it was too cold for the chicks. She begged her parents could she please bring those chicks inside. She told me they reluctantly said yes. (Can you imagine 50 chicks inside the house? My mother told me the house was only 4 rooms and at that time there was at least 8 or 9 of them at home. That means several someones had to sleep in the same room with those stinky, cheeping chicks.)

    The only heat they had was a wood burning stove in the kitchen and an old kerosene heater in one of the bedrooms. My mother got her father to move the kerosene heater in the room with the chicks. Before she went to bed she thought the chicks were cold so she turned the heater up. She then went to bed and went to sleep.

    In the wee hours of the night she was awakened

by shouting and scurrying people. The house was on fire!

My mother got caught up in helping the younger ones get out and then she remembered her chicks. She tried to get to their room but one of her brothers caught her .

"Let me go. I've got to git to my chicks."

"No, the heater in there is what caused the fire. Come on."

My mother allowed her brother to pull her out. She knew what really caused the fire. She had. She believed and still believes she caused her family's house to burn to the ground because she wanted to make sure her chicks were warm enough. She said that her family lost most of all their belongings. I always feel so sad for my mother for that. I can't imagine losing everything in a fire or any other way. When I was little our chimney caught on fire and we had a little damage but we didn't lose anything. It is sad to think of anyone, especially someone you know, losing everything.

Jeff Cavaness

Hog Hollow

I HATE SNAKES

One thing you need to know about me, I HATE SNAKES. Riley Washington Standfield and snakes do not git along well together. I know, I know, they serve their purpose but as far as I'm concerned they can serve their purpose away from me somewhere else.

Now that's that said, I want to tell you about one particular day that how I feel about snakes truly came to a screaming climax. (Climax, now that's an interesting word. Say it out loud and see what you think.)

As I have probably said before and will probably say again, living on the farm, I had chores to do. Feeding the pigs was a high priority for me and I had to do it every day. We had two corncribs. (For you city folk, a corncrib is where you store corn until you need it to have for your pigs.) Since we had different pigs in different lots I would take my bucket and fill it up with corn how ever many times I needed to feed that specific group of pigs. That day was no different. I headed for the first corn crib and climbed in and started picking up corn and putting it in my bucket. It was fairly dark in this particular crib but I had been in there millions of times so I wasn't particularly worried about finding my way.

It was towards the end of the summer and the corncribs were getting fairly empty so I was working in the crib corner picking up corn. I was distracted and I went over the crib door looking out. I thought I had heard my name called. I hadn't

Hog Hollow

and when I turned around, I about fainted. Right where I was fixin' to stick my hand was a snake. It was just sitting there, probably waiting for a mouse or something but the point was because it was dark, I didn't see it until I stepped back and that let some light shine on the snake. Needless to say, I don't know if that bunch of pigs got enuf to eat that night.

Irritated and shaken, I knew I had to go to the other corncrib and feed those pigs. I cautiously walked in. You know, I find a snake in one corncrib and it only goes to reason that I would find another one in the other crib. I walked in and didn't say anything. I let out a deep breath and started getting my corn. This crib was even emptier than the first one. I got my bucket full and turned around. You know what I saw. On the wall behind me, right where I had just walked, was a snake. The snake was hanging on the wall and it was between me and door. I just went out the window. By this time, I didn't care of those pigs got anything to eat ever.

Jeff Cavaness

PLUCKING CHICKENS

Have you ever plucked a chicken? (For all you city folks, plucking a chicken means gitting rid of all the chicken's feathers.)

Have you ever been around anywhere close when someone else was plucking a chicken? Well, if'n you haven't, you have not missed a thing.

Plucking a chicken is messy stinky work. I

only had to do it a few times and I never want to do it again ever. I guess if I was hungry and the only way for me to eat was to pluck a chicken, I would but I wouldn't want to.

I remember one time my parents decided we had too many chickens.

So they decided we would kill several of them and get them ready for cooking but put them in the freezer. Okay, I didn't have a problem with that until I was told what my part was going to be. I was not happy with my assignment.

The plan was to wait until dark and the chickens would be asleep. We would grab them and my daddy would cut their heads off. Have you ever seen a chicken with its head cut off? Have you ever heard the expression, "I was running around like a chicken with its head cut off"? Well, this is where that expression came from. (I guess it's a country expression.)

The next step was to grab the dead chicken by the feet and put them into a scalding pot of water. This was to help soften the skin and feathers.

Hog Hollow

Apparently, I was told, this would make plucking much easier. (I was all for that. Anything to make this job easier was okay with me.)

After a few minutes in the hot water, the chicken was pulled out and the plucking started. My job was pull the wet chicken out of the hot water and start plucking.

You know, chickens don't smell all that good anyway and being wet and dead does not make a chicken smell any better. In fact, it smells a lot worse. Wet feathers are stinky beyond words.

So here's the picture. I'm having to stick my hands down into a scalding pot of water to grab a dead, stinky chicken. Am I having fun? I won't answer. I think you get the picture.

I thought that night would never end. I don't think I actually had to pluck that many chickens but at the time any was too many.

I love fried chicken. But you know, if the only way I could get to eat it would be to go through this process every time, I might change my mind.

Jeff Cavaness

THE BACK PORCH SNAKE

Snakes are a very important part of nature. They are especially important on the farm. I'm talking about, what we called, chicken snakes. They were harmless to people, unless they were cornered. They ate pests like rats and mice. My daddy actually liked having them around the barn because of that fact. For instance, he made that statement to a farmer friend of his and that farmer brought him a big, long chicken snake for the barn. I didn't know this until it was already done but I didn't like it but there was nothing I could do or say. Personally, it was my experience that we had way too many snakes as it was.

One day I came home and saw that the back door of our house had been torn off the hinges. I didn't see anyone around. There was no one in the house or anywhere outside that I could see. The back porch was torn up too with everything thrown around. Our back porch had our freezer and a huge barrel of dog food and other junk that we couldn't find any other place to put.

Later on that evening my mother came in and I met her at the door and asked her what had happened. I followed her into the kitchen and she sat down.

"Riley, I want to tell you something."

My curiosity was up. What had happened that was causing my mother is act so seriously.

"Riley, the reason that door was off the hinges was that your daddy knocked it off."

"What was he doing? Did he fall through it or what?"

"Riley, we know how you feel about snakes."

I started getting a prickly feeling. What was going on?

"Your daddy came in to get some food for the dogs. He noticed the snake had wrapped itself around the base of the barrel and was probably waiting for a mice to come by or something."

I was not interested in wanting to know why the snake was there. I was interested in, "THERE WAS A SNAKE IN MY HOUSE!"

"Riley, calm down. It's gone. It was so big that that's how the door got torn off in the process of your daddy getting it out of the house. We didn't want to tell you but with the door being off, I knew we would have to tell you something."

"THERE WAS A SNAKE IN MY HOUSE!" I wasn't interested in any of the details. What was I going to do. Snakes in the yard and in and around the barn was one thing but snakes in my house was completely different. My mother was right about one thing, they knew how I felt about snakes and knew if I had found the snake, I would moved out letting the snake have the house and everything in it.

"Is it dead?"

"Dead as a doornail. It was almost 18 feet long. That's how it could wrap itself around the dog food barrel so many times."

I looked at her. I didn't care about how long it was. "THERE WAS A SNAKE IN MY HOUSE!"

MY DUCK

I have always thought ducks were cool birds. They had feathers and could swim. How cool it that! When I was round 12 years old someone gave me a duck. I was so excited! Now I could look at the duck, watch the duck, feed the duck and generally just have a duck as a pet.

As you can guess, it didn't work out quite that way.

First, that duck didn't have any interest in being my or anyone else's pet. All that duck wanted to do was eat and sleep. Now I know that most animals' purpose in life was to eat and sleep but this was my duck. I wanted to watch my duck swim in the pond. Was that too much to ask? I just wanted to see him swim around in our pond.

I cannot tell you how many times I chased that duck trying to make it go into the water. I would run and yell and even on occasion, throw things to make that stupid duck go into the water. Looking back, maybe it was me who was the stupid one. Who knows what could have been in that pond.

We had snakes and turtles and who know what else living in our ponds and maybe the duck knew something I didn't. At the time though, I didn't think or care about any of that. I wanted that duck to swim and I wanted to be able to watch it swim.

Well, chasing it didn't work. Spying on it hoping I could catch it swimming didn't work. I finally decided that my duck was a non-swimming duck. I finally gave up.

Hog Hollow

Let me tell you what my duck did like to do. Remember I told you that all the duck liked to do was eat and sleep. That duck would stay in the pigpens and eat pig food and even sleep with the pigs. I believe that duck believed he was a pig. Every time I looked for that duck, he was eating alongside the pigs. Needless to say, that duck got fat and waddled more than most ducks.

I eventually gave up trying to make that duck swim and I got interested in something else. One day I was at the barn doing my chores and got to thinking that I hadn't seen the duck lately. I got to looking and finally found it. The duck was dead. He was close to one of the pig troughs. It looked like the duck had gotten so fat he couldn't stay out of the pigs' way.

The pigs probably ran over it trampling it to death.

I looked at the duck and was sad. You know, I really wanted to watch that duck swim.

Jeff Cavaness

THE COW AND THE ELECTRIC FENCE

Cows are perhaps the stupidest animals on earth. You don't believe me, just try to get them to do something you want. Did you know that if easy food is available cows will eat until they founder themselves? This could kill them.

But apparently, they don't care. They want to eat. They just look at you and chew their cuds.

Jeff Cavaness

You know, when I was little, that cud chewing used to fascinate me. I just couldn't understand what they could be chewing for such a long time. I knew that cows didn't chew bubble gum. I just couldn't figure it out.

You know the Standfields' were pig farmers but we also had a few head of cattle too along. Thirty to forty cows was the maximum we ever on the place at any given time. Actually, before I was born my parents kept some milk cows and sold milk everyday. A milk truck would come around and collect the milk and take it to the milk factory, I guess. By the time I was old enough to be of any help in that department, my parents stopped selling milk. My daddy said it was too much trouble for not enough money.

I used to name all the cows. I could chart their family tree. I never did that with the pigs. Too hard when you're talking about hundreds of pigs. But I could tell you which calves went with which cow and which cows were sisters and stuff like that. It was fun to watch a baby calf grow and find its way within it's own family. Of course, when you get that interested in any animal, it hurts when it is sold away from you. But that's part of living on a working farm.

Electric fences came to our part of the country very slowly. It wasn't that the farmers didn't want them. It just was that they were a little difficult to make sure they worked correctly and all the time. If one thin blade of grass or one little stick touched the wire, the rest of the fence was inoperable. (Inoperable – that's one of those words that makes you sound smart.) Electric fences could be great. My daddy could see the potential it had but he was very slow to put one to use. I remember going over to one of my uncles' farms to check out his new electric fence. It looked so innocent and looked like it wouldn't keep any animal or anything in. Don't make the mistake of touching it to find out. If you do, you will find out real quick that it is real and is quite capable of deterring anyone or anything and please, oh please, take my word for it. Do not, I repeat, do not pee on the fence.

If you do, you will regret for a long time after the fact.

Now, to put the cow and the electric fence together at the same time.

What convinced my daddy to put in an electric fence was one particular cow.

Next to one of our cow pastures was a cornfield. Now, the grass in the pasture was fine. There was plenty of it and it was fresh and everything a cow could want. What this particular cow wanted was in the cornfield. Before the electric fence the cow would break into the cornfield. We would get her out and fix the fence. The next day she would do it again. After a couple of weeks of this my daddy decided to give the electric fence a try. We worked on getting the fence row cleared so that nothing would touch the wire. We got it up and my daddy switched it on. We sat back to see what would happen with us out of the way. I told you cows were stupid. This old cow went over to the fence and she couldn't see us anywhere around. She started to poke her head through and when she got her body close enough to the wire, all of a sudden she jerked and ran back halfway across the pasture. My daddy and I just laughed and laughed.

We got a bigger laugh when we saw that stupid cow go back and try it again.

This time she ran farther way across the pasture. I told you cows were stupid.

You know, that cow never gave us another problem when it came to getting into where she wasn't supposed to be. Even still, my daddy never really used the electric fences much. He said they were just too much trouble. I don't know, except from the peeing part, I thought they were a lot of fun when people and animals didn't know they were there.

Jeff Cavaness

TYLER'S STORE

Nowadays, most communities have at least one store if not three or four. When I was a little boy we had one store, Old Man Tyler's Store. You know, I never heard it called anything but that. I guess Old Man Tyler's Store was the official name.

Old Man Tyler's Store was the Wal-Mart of Hog Holler. Old Man Tyler's Store had everything.

Jeff Cavaness

Remember, we lived way out in the country and once a week my parents made a trip to town to shop. If we needed anything between trips to town, we went to Old Man Tyler's Store.

Old Man Tyler had run the store forever or at least as long as anybody could remember. The store set in a crossroads and was a gathering place for the neighborhood. Each and every time you went there you'd find at least two or three farmers talking (gossiping) and generally wasting time. The only problem with Tyler's was that Old Man Tyler never, I said never, threw anything away. Of course, foodstuffs and milk would get replaced but nothing else.

I loved going to Old Man Tyler's Store. You never knew what you'd find. But that had its drawbacks. I have bought candy and got it home and unwrapped it and discovered it was old and way past time it should have been eaten.

One day I had saved up some money and when I got the opportunity I went to Old Man Tyler's Store ready to spend my money. As my Mother used to say, "That money was just burning a hole in his pocket!" I busily looked up and down the aisles looking for that special treat. My eyes suddenly saw a box of balloons. I love balloons. (I still love balloons and my little boy loves balloons too.) I grabbed a handful, paid for them and excitedly waited to get home. When I did I immediately took out my new balloons and proceeded to blow one up. It exploded in my face. Okay, so what, I got one bad balloon. Guess what? All of them was bad. Every single balloon exploded when I tried to blow them up. I was so upset. Then I got mad!

How dare Old Man Tyler! Money for me is hard to come by and to let me buy old rotten balloons is terrible!

I decided I was not going to stand for it. I determined that I had paid for good balloons and I was going to get some good balloons. The very next day I got my chance. I was back at Old Man Tyler's Store and I took the same number of balloons I had bought the day before. (Yeah, I technically stole 'em but what's right is right. He should have thrown the old ones away. Shouldn't he?)

I got home with them and thoroughly enjoyed playing with those balloons. You know, I was always very careful of what I bought at Old Man Tyler's Store after that. In fact, I never bought another balloon there again.

(Just so you'll know, I know stealing is wrong and I am a very honest person. I also figured out that more than likely, Old Man Tyler would have probably given me new balloons if I had told him what happened but when you're very young, all you think about is the injustice of things sometimes.)

PLAYING IN THE FLOOD

Growing up I had plenty of toys and my son now has more toys than he can play with. But as I remember my childhood so many of my most fun times were when I was just out playing in the yard or in the pig lots.

Did you get outside and play in the rain when you were little? Of course, if it was thundering and lightening you couldn't but otherwise you could. I did. I would strip off my shoes and socks and that wasn't even a problem most of the summer. I would go barefoot all the time. Some times during the summer the only time I would wear shoes would be to church.

Actually one summer I didn't even wear shoes to church for a while because at the beginning of summer I stepped on a bee and my foot swelled up on me and I couldn't get my shoe on. It was so much fun going to church barefoot it was almost worth getting stung by the bee. (Well, almost.)

Between our house and one of the pig barns was a small creek. Now, I hesitate to call it a creek because the majority of the time the only thing that was in it was dirt. But if rained enough sometimes a small flow of water would be there for a short time. Occasionally if we had a big rain for a long time, it would swell up to probably over 20 feet wide. That was when it was dangerous. Remember, those hogs still had to be fed. They didn't care how much it had rained. They were hungry. When I was little I didn't have to try to get across because my daddy would go feed those particular hogs at that barn. We had other barns with pigs to feed that you didn't have to get across a wide section of water.

My mother was always worried that I would get in the water and get swept away. I guess she was right. A lot of people misjudge water and drown all the time. And little kids don't usually think about stuff like that anyway.

But watching that fast flowing water was fascinating to me. It was exciting to watch and it was right in my own back yard. Of course, occasionally I would see some animal that that been caught up stream and drowned but not usually. That would make me sad but would remind me of the danger.

When I got older I would venture out and try to cross without being knocked off my feet. Once I did get knocked over and went under the water for a second. It wasn't a big deal because I was big enough to deal with it but it taught me a lesson to pay attention to what was happening and could happen. I loved to play in the water though.

There was one down side to being able to cross. I had to help feed the hogs on that side of the creek. Oh well, being able to do things brings with it responsibilities. I had fun though. Nowadays there are probably all kinds pesticides and trash being washed along someone could become deathly ill just playing in their backyard creek.

You know, I still go barefoot every chance I get. My son is the same way. I guess you can't take away the "country genes".

SLEEPY HOLLOW

The other legend concerns a road called Sleepy Hollow. Remember, this ain't the north. That lame story about some headless horseman riding down some sleepy hollow is completely different from my story.

Sleepy Hollow road was a gravel road with so many curves and hills and dips you'd swear you were in the mountains. Remember, I lived close to the Mississippi River and there ain't no mountains anywhere close.

We would go through Sleepy Hollow every once in a while. It was very wooded and dark for most of the drive. I loved going through there and I would ask my mother or father to tell me the stories that surrounded Sleepy Hollow. There were some old houses that nobody lived in and, in my opinion, should have been torn down. There is nothing worse than seeing a house that's not being lived in. It just looks lonely and desolate. Add that to a place that is dark with tall trees everywhere and you have the setting for some really spooky tales.

Every year someone would get the bright idea to go camp out at one of those deserted old houses. There would be stories of odd and strange lights and noises coming from seemingly nowhere.

The strangest and to me, the funniest story concerned some of my cousins. Three of my male cousins, all older than me, decided to spend

Hog Hollow

the night at one of those ramshackle houses in Sleepy Hollow. I remember thinking that these particular cousins were not the smartest cousins I had.

The night they picked was cool and clear. It was October if I remember correctly. They planned on getting there before it got dark and gathering a lot of wood for a fire. (To me, having the fire would have been the best part. From what I heard, I think that before the night was finished they thought the fire was the best part of the night too.)

They took their sleeping bags and planned on having some fun and showing everybody how brave they were. My cousin, Sammy, was always a big talker. You couldn't believe a word he said. He probably is still that a way. He had been bragging for days about how him and his brothers, Stu and Shorty, would spend the night in Sleepy Hollow and they weren't afraid of nothing. (My aunt liked names that began with S.) That night they were so full of themselves. They had stopped off by our house on they're way trying to get my brother to go with them. My brother was a little older than them and I like to think, a lot smarter. Anyway, he told them he had other plans and for them to have fun. You should of heard them brag and talk about how big and bad they were because they were going to show everybody there wasn't anything to be afraid of in Sleepy Hollow.

At our house that night we got our chores done and we went on to bed like every other night. Early the next morning we heard the biggest racket you ever heard. Sammy was yelling and pounding on our back door. (One fact you need to know. Our house was the first house of relatives they could get to after leaving Sleepy Hollow.)

My father ran to the door in his underwear and pulled it open.

"Sammy, what are you yelling about? What's going on?"

Sammy and his brothers almost fell in the room. By that time me and my brother and mother had gotten there too. Those boys looked like they were half dead. And they were all talking at once. Each one was trying to be heard over the other. Finally, my father had had enough.

"Boys!" He shouted. And when my father wanted to be heard, you could hear him.

"Boys, what's going on? Only one of you talk at a time. Sammy?"

All three stopped and Stu and Shorty both looked at Sammy.

"Sammy?" My father asked again.

Sammy looked around at each of us. He looked white as a sheet.

They all three did. I remember thinking how funny this would have been if all three of them didn't look so scared.

My mother went over to Sammy. She took his hand. "Come on, Sammy, take a deep breath and tell us what's going on." My mother was great. She could always calm me down if I was upset. She did the same thing for Sammy and all of them.

Sammy started his story.

"You know, we left here and got to the old house. We gathered a big pile of wood and got our beds ready and started the fire and went over to explore that old house. You know, we've been in it before but at twilight it looked different. We looked around but we didn't seen anything different from what we've seen before, maybe more dirt and spider webs."

I could tell Sammy was starting to calm down. He had an audience, why not. His brothers on the other hand seemed about ready to jump out of their pants.

"We went on back outside and got on our sleeping bags and took out some food to eat. By now it was gitting dark. As we started eatin' we heard a low sound that sounded a lot like a growl come from the direction of the house. We looked at each other and looked at the house. Nothing. We started back to eat. Again, the growl sounded but this time it was louder.

We got up. We weren't scared yet. You know, who knows what it could be out there in the woods."

Shorty jumped up. "I told them we should go home but they wouldn't listen to me?"

Sammy pulled Shorty down. "Shut up, Shorty! Let me go on."

Shorty just looked at him.

Stu looked at Sammy. "Go on, Sammy, tell them the rest of it."

"Okay, okay. We decided to go look in the house. If it was some animal or something, we needed to scare it off or kill it one. We started towards the house. All of a sudden we heard a third growl and this one was louder than any of the others. We stopped and looked around."

Shorty yelled, "I was ready to go home!"

Stu, "Shorty, sit down and let Sammy go on."

Sammy glared at Shorty.

"Before we could decide what to do. The growl started again and it sounded like it was moving. It stopped. The next time we heard it was on the opposite side of the fire away from the house. We decided to go back to the fire."

My brother asked a question. "Sammy, did you find out what made the sound?"

"No, that's what so weird. Nothing that followed helped us figure out where that sound was coming from."

"We got back to the fire and we never heard the growl again. After a little while we calmed down some and decided to roast wieners over the fire.

We had already gotten some sticks so we got 'em over the fire when the wind started blowing hard."

My father interrupted. "There was no wind last night."

Shorty jumped in. "There was where we was at."

"The wind was so hard it was blowing leaves and brush at us from all directions. I thought the fire was going to go out it was blowing so hard.

We worked hard running around trying to keep our stuff from flying away and about the time we decided to make a run for the truck, the wind completely stopped. It was so still I believe you could of heard something from miles away."

We all looked at each other. I was wondering just what had happened out there. I don't think my brother completely believed them and I don't think my father did either. I don't know about my mother.

"What happened next?" my mother asked.

Sammy continued. "We got everything back right and we talked about leaving but we decided to stay."

Stu and Shorty both jumped in. "He decided to stay. We didn't have a choice!"

I swear I saw my father and mother both trying not to laugh. It was pretty funny.

Sammy glared at his brothers. "We decided to stay. We were there to prove that nothing strange happened in Sleepy Hollow."

I couldn't help myself. "You mean, you weren't convinced yet."

My mother touched my arm. "Riley, let Sammy finish."

"We got everything down and we looked around but didn't see anything out of the ordinary so we settled back down to eat. We ate and nothing else happened. We decided to try to get some sleep. The fire had burned down so we put some more wood on it to get the flames high. I guess we all went to sleep."

Stu and Shorty nodded. Shorty added, "It weren't easy."

My mother smiled.

"Like I said, we finally fell asleep and all was okay until about 3 o'clock I guess. I couldn't see my watch very clearly but I knew it was past midnight."

I asked, "What happened at 3?"

Sammy looked like he was starting to enjoy this whole story telling thing. It made me wonder just how true it was.

"Something woke me up. I don't know what. I laid there for a while and then I heard that same low growl we had heard earlier. I reached over and shook Stu and Shorty to wake them up. I told them I heard something.

About the time I got 'em up we heard the sound again. Then Stu shouted, "Look over there!" In the distance was something glowing. We stood up.

The light seemed to be coming closer. Then the growl started again and it too was coming from the same direction of the light. The light started bouncing and every time the light seemed to bounce on the ground, we heard the growl. It started gitting closer and closer."

Sammy's voice was gitting louder and louder. He had jumped up and was wildly moving his arms around. Stu and Shorty seemed to be gitting more nervous.

My father reached up to Sammy, "Steady, just tell us what happened then."

Sammy's eyes had gotten big just like he was reliving the whole thing.

"Like I said the light and growl was gitting closer. We looked around at each other and tried to see anything. Then the light and sound changed directions. It started coming from behind that old house. We still couldn't see much of anything. Then," Sammy looked like he was gitting more and more excited. "Then, the light seemed to fill the house so that each window in that old house seemed to pour light out. The growling sound got louder and louder. The light got brighter and brighter. We started edging toward the truck. All of a sudden the light seemed to explode out of that house. It started gitting closer and closer to us. The growl was louder and was coming with it." Sammy stopped. He seemed too tired to go on.

My brother jumped up shouting, "Don't stop! What happened then?"

Sammy took a deep breath. "That light came towards us and that growl seemed to git louder. Then the wind started blowing like it had last night. What with the light, the growl and now the wind, that was too much.

We ran and jumped in the truck. The wind was blowing so hard we could feel it shaking the truck.

We put the windows up. The windows started rattling. The light got closer and closer. It went through the fire and when it passed through the fire, it put the fire out. The growl was still getting louder and louder. Even inside the truck it was loud. Shorty and Stu was shouting at me to start the truck but I couldn't. I was watching the light. It was like I was paralyzed. It came right up to the truck and seemed to stop. The growl stopped too. Then all of a sudden the light and growl seemed to come through the truck and us and went out the other side. We watched it go into the woods on the other side of the field and disappear. I got the key in the ignition and I floored it and we didn't slow down "til we got here."

With that all the life seemed to go out of Sammy. He slumped down on our couch. My mother just smiled at us and patted his hand. I looked at Stu and Shorty. They seemed drained too. Nobody said nothing. My mother stood up.

"How about I fix everyone some breakfast?"

Everyone nodded and she went to the kitchen

and soon you could hear pots and pans rattling and breakfast smells coming out.

My father looked at my cousins. "Anything else? Anything you want to tell us?"

I looked at my father. Didn't he believe my cousins? I knew I was inclined to not believe but I never cared much for these cousins. They were always too loud and bragging about stuff that I didn't believe anybody could brag about. I looked at my brother. I wondered if he believed them or not.

Sammy looked at my father. "I have never been so scared in all my life. I never want to even think about Sleepy Hollow again let alone go there."

Nothing else was really ever said about it. Breakfast was eaten in near silence and my cousins left to go home. You know, I never did hear of them talking much about that night ever again. Maybe it did happen, who knows.

You know, I always wanted to ask them what ever happened to their sleeping bags and did they ever go back to Sleepy Hollow.

GRASSHOPPER

Before you start assuming anything, Grasshopper was a horse. He was a beautiful horse called an Appaloosa. If you don't know what an Appaloosa looks like, remember those old westerns that used to be on television. A lot of the times the Indians rode Appaloosas. They can be distinguished from other horses by their markings. Appaloosas had spots on half their bodies and the rest of their bodies were a solid color, usually brown. Grasshopper was brown with white spots.

Grasshopper was a beautiful horse but there is something else you need to know about Grasshopper. He was mean. I don't know if he had been mistreated before my brother got him or he just naturally had a mean disposition. My experience and knowledge of horses is not on the same level as my experience with pigs and cows.

About the only person Grasshopper would let come near him was my brother which was a good thing considering it was my brother who owned him and bought him to ride. I never got too close after I saw Grasshopper in action around my father and any of my brother's friends. I thought to myself that no matter how much I might want to help with Grasshopper it wasn't worth getting kicked or bitten. (You know, I think that was pretty smart thinking for a 10 year old.)

Speaking of my brother's friends brings me

back to a story. My brother had a friend named Roger. Roger might have been my brother's friend but that didn't make him a favorite with my parents or me. Roger was just one of those guys you just automatically disliked. He was a know-it-all about any subject you might bring up. He was better at anything he tried than anyone else in the world according to him. I just didn't like him and I tried my best to not be where he was at.

One day Roger stopped by our house to see my brother. My brother wasn't there. My mother stepped out on the porch to talk to Roger. (Do you think my mother didn't want Roger in the house? I didn't.)

"Roger, Carter's not home." (Carter was my brother's name. Carter was named after someone in my mother's family. Carter was a family name that had been passed down.)

"Mrs. Standfield, I just wanted to ride a little while. I just thought I would stop and see if Carter wanted to go riding too."

"Roger, I'm sorry, I don't know when Carter'll

be back."

Roger looked around towards the barn and then turned back to my mother.

"Mrs. Standfield, do you think it would be all right if I rode a little while anyway?"

My mother thought a minute.

"Sure, Roger, that'll be okay. Just be sure none of the horses get out.

Carter'll got one or two who really like to get through the gate before you notice what they're doing."

"Thanks. I'll be careful."

I was watching from the window and heard all this. I watched Roger head towards the horse barn. My mother and I thought he would pick one of the other horses but Roger went for Grasshopper. I thought we might need to warn him about Grasshopper but I decided since he was friends with my brother he probably knew all about all the horses.

To his credit, Roger did know about Grasshopper but he decided he would ride him anyway. Remember what I said about Roger, he knew everything and he was the best at anything and everything.

Somehow Roger got Grasshopper saddled and ready to be ridden.

This was not easy but Roger had him cornered and could control him better in the barn. This was not the case when Roger led Grasshopper out of the barn. He led Grasshopper out into the front yard of our house. By now my mother is standing there watching too.

Roger got on Grasshopper. Grasshopper just stood there. Roger tried to make Grasshopper go forward. Grasshopper just stood there. (I decided I kind of liked Grasshopper.) Roger started yelling at Grasshopper.

Grasshopper just looked bored. Roger started gouging/kicking Grasshopper.

This got Grasshopper's attention. Grasshopper took a few steps forward and all of a sudden he started bucking hard. After two or three bucks Roger goes flying onto the ground. I started laughing. My mother looked at me hard.

She had been watching too.

"Riley, he could be hurt." (I noticed she didn't hurry out to see if he was hurt.)

I looked at my mother. I swear she was having a hard time herself not laughing.

"Look, Mother, he's getting up."

Roger got up and started walking toward Grasshopper. I do think Grasshopper was laughing at Roger himself. He allowed Roger to catch him and climb back up on top of him. (I think Grasshopper was toying with Roger.)

As soon as Roger was up seated on Grasshopper started bucking again and again Roger went flying. This time both my mother and me started laughing.

When Roger got up this time he went over to a bush and cut himself a switch. He grabbed Grasshopper by the halter and started beating him on his head and neck. My mother started toward the door to stop him. Before she could say anything Roger jumped up on top of Grasshopper and started kicking and yelling again. Grasshopper started bucking but this time he was bucking sideways and backwards. This time was different for Roger too.

He stayed on this time.

I guess Grasshopper got tired of fooling with Roger because he stopped and just stood there. Roger had a great smile on his face. I thought he believed he had won. I could hear him bragging that he could ride any horse. Personally, just sitting on a horse didn't mean you rode that horse to me. I think to qualify as riding you need to cover some ground while on the horse's back.

Anyway, while Roger was sitting there on Grasshopper he was just grinning. Grasshopper on the other hand didn't look too happy. All of a sudden Grasshopper started bucking and reared up trying to throw Roger off.

It didn't work. Roger is still grinning. Grasshopper rared up one more time and this time didn't come down. He went over backwards trying to roll over on Roger. Roger did have enough sense to jump off. Roger was not grinning any longer.

You know, Roger didn't try to get on Grasshopper ever again. He took Grasshopper back to the barn and unsaddled him and let him go. He went and got in his truck and left. He didn't say anything to us or nothing.

I decided that Grasshopper was a great horse. You know, Grasshopper received a little extra supper that night. I decided Grasshopper needed a little reward. Grasshopper did a lot of good for us. Roger didn't come over to house near as much. You know, I think horses deserve more credit for being excellent judges of character.

THE CAR WRECK

I've told you some about learning to drive growing up in Hog Holler but let me tell you about my first and worst car wreck.

I got my drivers' license in September of my 16th year. On Halloween that year I begged my parents to let me and my friend, Kyle, go riding around.

They thought about it but ultimately decided to

not let me. My daddy talked to me about it.

"Riley, I really don't want you out in the car on Halloween. Some people are so stupid on that night. I think it might be too dangerous driving around.

Why don't you and Kyle go out Saturday night and do something? You can have the car that night."

I knew I wasn't going to win so I agreed and on Saturday night I picked Kyle up and we drove off talking about what we could get into. We didn't have anything in mind specifically. We just knew we wanted to have some fun. My daddy's only advice had been to stay off the main roads because he believed the main roads would have more traffic and people would drive faster on the main roads. (I wondered then if my daddy remembered being 16.)

Now, the story I'm about to tell you is the truth. The story we told our parents and anybody else who asked was quite different. As you can guess from the title is that I did have a car accident that

Hog Hollow

night. What you don't know is what led up to the wreck. We let everyone believe I was driving on the back road and was driving too fast and lost control of the car and turned over. The result was that my daddy's car was totaled.

This is the true story.

On the first Saturday after Halloween Kyle and I jumped into my daddy's car and set out to have some fun. Now, what that "fun" was we didn't know, we just knew that we had a car and a full tank of gas and we were going to have fun.

We drove around for a while talking and I was staying on the back roads mostly to make my daddy happy in case he asked. (He would to.) We had brought some fireworks left over from Halloween with us. The fireworks consisted mostly of firecrackers and actually we didn't have that many. I had brought them along for no reason in particular. Anyway, we happened to turn down this road that had a guy from my school (Kyle and I went to different school but both of us went to Standfield Chapel Presbyterian Church.) lived at.

I didn't like him and Kyle knew him too and didn't like him either. We drove past his house and starting talking about him and after we got down the road past his house, we got a seemingly brilliant idea. Kyle and I decided to blow up this guy's mailbox. (Now you know why I'm telling the truth after 20 years.)

This was the plan. Kyle got in the back seat of my car. He rolled his window down so he could put the firecrackers in the mailbox, light the fuse and then close the lid. I then would get us away from the front of the house as fast as possible. You know, it didn't happen that way.

What did happen was that Kyle did get in the back seat and roll his window down. He did put the firecrackers in the mailbox and light the fuse.

He then yelled.

"Riley, get us out of here!"

I slammed on the accelerator and got us going. Now comes the interesting part. We were on a gravel road. (Remember my daddy told me to stay off the main highways.) The gravel road

Hog Hollow

had just been graded. (For all you city folks, when a gravel road is graded the gravel is smoothed out and usually there is pile of gravel on each side of the road.) This is the way it was on this particular gravel road. When I had pulled over in front of the mailbox I had pulled over into the fresh pile of gravel. When Kyle yelled at me to move and I slammed on the accelerator the fresh gravel and my inexperience as a driver caused me to lose control and I ended up in the ditch on the left side of the road. I got us out of that ditch and was headed across the road straight for one of the biggest oak trees I have ever seen. I slammed on the brakes but missed the brakes and hit the accelerator. This caused the car to try to climb the big oak tree and the car rolled over three times before stopping.

This was the day before seat belts so neither Kyle or I was protected in that way. When we finally stopped Kyle popped his window that was down and started running. He looked back to see if I was behind him. I wasn't. He ran back.

"Riley, come on. The car is going to blow up!" (It never did.)

I didn't answer. I had hit my head in the collision.

"Riley, come on!" Kyle was yelling and yelling. I finally got my senses back together to answer him.

"Kyle, I can't get out."

"Riley, roll back and come out the back window."

The car was still running even though it was upside down. I did have enough sense to reach up and turn the ignition off. I then somehow got back to the window and crawled out. When I tried to stand up I discovered I had hurt my knee. I could hardly walk. Kyle helped me and we walked and hopped to a house about half a mile down the road. We definitely didn't want to go to the house where we had just blown up the mailbox. I had to lean on Kyle for part of the way. We got to the house, which happened to be a preacher's house, and called our parents.

Hog Hollow

You know, right after the wreck Kyle was very calm and I was slightly hysterical but the longer we waited the calmer I got and Kyle got visibly more upset. Everything turned out all right and I still have a bad knee because of it but I learned something very important: Don't drive around on the back roads.

Worst of all though, we went through all that for nothing. When Kyle had lit the firecrackers' fuse, he yelled for me to go. One important thing he forgot, he didn't close the mailbox lid. The firecrackers just blew out. As far as I know no one ever knew what we tried to do. You know, that's probably for the best.

We were mean and destructive boys. We just thought it would be fun. I doubt very seriously if Kyle had remembered to close the lid if there would have been any damage anyway.

I finally told my mother the truth about the wreck about ten years later. I wasn't taking any chances. Actually, I'm not too sure about telling you now.

Jeff Cavaness

But I think I'm fairly safe. You know, that boy's house we were at was not in Standfield Chapel. If it had of been, I probably would not have survived to tell you about it now.

HALLOWEEN

I know that Halloween is celebrated in many different ways, probably in as many different ways as there are different communities. In Standfield Chapel we celebrated by having a church Halloween party and then going trick or treating. When you got too old to trick or treat, you just went tricking. Now, tricking in Standfield Chapel consisted of toilet papering someone's yard or soaping some windows, you know, tame stuff like that. I think the wildest thing I was ever party to was we put a NO DUMPING sign on the front porch of Standfield Chapel Presbyterian Church.

One particular Halloween night I begged and pleaded enuf to get my brother and his wife to let me go with them around doing stuff. When you go tricking in the country, you do it on foot. You also have to take care that no one sees you. Anyway, for a little boy this can be very exciting. On the one hand I was excited to be out with the "big kids" and on the other hand I was excited to be part of doing something besides tricking and treating.

As the night passed we dodged vehicles on the road so as not to be seen.

We toilet papered a couple of yards and generally did harmless things. Now when you toilet paper someone's yard, it's easier to do it when they're not home. The danger and exciting part is when you do it when someone is home.

My brother decided we need to toilet paper

this particular house. It belonged to one of the few families that was not kin to the Standfields'. I don't know why my brother wanted to do this but it was all right with me. I was having fun. He was the grownup in the situation. Let's do it!

We got started. We tried very hard to do a good job but at the same time not make any noises. Well, you and I both know, that's not possible. We were about three quarters done when the front door flew open and out rushes three big guys. They are yelling at us and we take off.

Apparently, they only see my brother and take out after him. My brother's wife and I happen to run to hide in the same place and it is in the opposite direction of where they are running and shouting looking for my brother. We get the idea of throwing rocks back at the barn where the rocks clatter and make noise on its tin roof. We throw the rocks anywhere we can where we think they will make noise. We move our position and throw rocks.

After about 15 minutes of this the three guys

Jeff Cavaness

are totally confused. They can't find the person they saw and then they hear all kinds of racket coming from behind and beside their house. They try to find what's making the noise but finally give up.

They go back in the house and close the door. We wait a few minutes and head for home. I won't say that Halloween is my favorite but I will say it was one of the most exciting.

THE TRAILOR PARK

As you have read, I live in Standfield Chapel. Now, Standfield Chapel is made up of mostly farms with farmhouses. There were a few houses just on small lots but mostly big farmhouses. Now I've said that I was kin to 99% of all the people who lived in Standfield Chapel so when a new family moved in, it was big news to everyone.

Now why someone who wasn't kin to the

Standfields' or a pig farmer would want to move to Standfield Chapel, I don't know. But one day a man came around and wanted to buy a lot for a house. About a mile from our house the farmer there, who by the way was one of the few who wasn't kin to the Standfields', sold him a lot on the paved road. We all waited to see when the house would be built. Not a lot of houses had been built in Standfield Chapel since I could remember so I was excited to see it done.

Finally, a bulldozer came worked on the lot to get it level. A plumbing guy came and dug the septic tank for their bathroom. The electric people came to run the lines. Next, nothing happened for what seemed like was a long time. Then one day I was out in our front yard playing when I saw this car with lights flashing coming down the road. Behind it was a big truck so wide it took up the entire road. The truck was carrying what looked like a square looking building. It had doors and windows and it dawned on me that it could be someone's house. I had heard about people moving houses, whole houses. I ran inside to tell my parents what was happening and they run out to see the truck pass. My daddy and I jumped into the car and followed at a safe distance. My daddy said,

"We don't want to get too close. That thing might slip off."

I didn't know one way or the other. I was just excited to be following it to see what was happening.

"You know what, Riley?"

"What Daddy?"

"I bet that thing belongs to those new folks what's moving in. What do you think?"

I didn't know what to think. I truly would have liked to get a look on the inside of that thing. We followed until we saw it stop in front of the new folk's lot. My daddy had been right. We parked and watched the truck back up and pull up and maneuver (Maneuver, that's a great word. Maneuver, say is out loud. It doesn't sound like what it is, does it.) trying to get that "house" on the property. They did and got it set up on blocks. We watched for a while and then went home.

"Riley, what'll you think about that? Would you like to live in one of those things?"

"I don't think so. I like our house and my grandparents' house but I don't think I would like living in that metal box. I like our house just fine."

My daddy laughed.

"I think they call it a trailer."

"I don't care what they call it. I'm glad we have our house.

"Me too, Riley, me too."

We went home and I went back to my playing wondering about that "trailer house".

What I didn't know was that my daddy's reaction was calm compared to others in Standfield Chapel. Some of my other relatives were not happy with the new "house" going up in Standfield Chapel. They thought it looked horrible and would only bring the property values down on the rest of our properties. At that time I didn't have a clue what a "property value" was but I did know they weren't happy.

We all continued to watch and talk about the new neighbors and their new "trailer house". You know, farm people don't like change and this new-fangled house trailer was not making my aunts and uncles very happy. A couple of my uncles actually went to talk to our new neighbor, a Mr. Scott, and asked him about his house and even went so far as to ask how long they would be staying the Standfield Chapel. He was told to mind his own business. That was a big mistake for someone new to do to someone in a community where everyone is kin to everyone else. The new neighbors were not making friends very fast. Now, I will admit to you that the new guy was right; it was none of my uncle's business. (Don't tell anyone I said that though.)

The ranting and raving finally died down when the Scott family moved in. They planted some trees and flowers and mowed their lawn. My family was at least pacified (Do you like that

Jeff Cavaness

word? It's a new one I just learned.) because they believed the new family was at least taking care of their yard. It was even suggested that maybe the Scott's couldn't afford to build a bigger house right now and anyone can understand someone wanting to have their own house. Then one day a couple of my aunts stopped by our house quite unexpectedly. I was outside when they drove up.

They yelled at me, "Riley, go git your parents. We want to talk to 'em."

I jumped up and ran inside. "Mama, Daddy, Aint Zola and Aint Vergie are outside. They want to talk to you. They seem awful upset."

My Mama and Daddy hurried outside to talk to my aunts. I hung back but I was close enough to hear. I knew something was up. I wanted to know what. The reason I was trying to stay out of the way was y family was bad about thinking that kids shouldn't be able to hear what grownups are discussing. And I had to hear what had my aunts so upset.

Hog Hollow

My Aint Zola was absolutely fuming, "Do you know what those Scott's have done now?"

Before either one of my parents could reply, My Aint Vergie was shouting too. "Those people have put old car tires on top of their trailer."

Aint Zola couldn't stop, "And they painted them white! What do you think about that?"

My parents looked at each other. I wondered if they were waiting to see if my aunts were through or not. My daddy opened his mouth to say something. He didn't get a chance. Aint Zola cut him off.

"Well, I can see you ain't in the least concerned. You don't to look out your kitchen window every blessed day and see that house contraption (I actually didn't know my aunt knew such a big word.) thing, trailer thing, house thing, do you. Well, I do! And I'm tired of it. (If you hadn't realized it yet, my Aint Zola lived across the road from the new neighbors. I have to admit that before the Scotts' moved in, Aint Zola had a great view that consisted of pastures and corn fields. That was a big difference from a trailer house with old tires on it's roof.)

"Aint Zola, what can we do about it? I don't like it any better than you do but what can we do?"

"I thought that be your attitude. Well, let me tell you one thing.

Don't come crying to me when Standfield Chapel becomes a big ole trailer park."

A trailer park, I wonder what that is. I guess I'll find out some day.

CAMPING

Right now, at this minute, I can tell you Riley Washington Standfield never plans on going camping ever again. Of course, my son and wife may have different plans of the future. We'll have to see.

One of the reasons for my attitude is my brother. Remember I told you I have an older brother, Carter, who loved to torment me at times.

Jeff Cavaness

I'll get back to him in a minute.

When I was an early teenager my friends and I loved to camp out over night. Our camping out consisted of rigging up some old tarpaulin on a couple of poles and building a big fire and playing around. Actually, if the truth be known, the camping out part was only so we could build a fire. Building a fire and watching it burn stuff was neat. It still is to this day. My family and I sometimes still build a fire out behind our house and sit around and roast hot dogs and marshmallows. It's a great time.

My friend Kyle and I decided we wanted to camp out one night. My daddy said okay but only if we camped out in front of the house off to the side.

Okay, we would agree to most anything to get to do it.

That afternoon we set up the so-called tent and gathered wood and food and got our sleeping stuff together. We even had a lantern that we used. We were really roughing it or so we thought. That night we played around with the fire and ate all

Hog Hollow

our food in the first hour and then sat around the campfire talking and poking at the fire. We sat there talking for a long time and about the time we were beginning to get sleepy out of the dark came two blood-curdling screams. We jumped up and looked at each other. All of a sudden out of the night two figures ran towards us yelling knocking us down. They grabbed our lantern and took off.

We got up and followed a short ways but couldn't see anything. I heard something. It was my brother laughing. Apparently, Carter and one of his buddies had decided to have a little fun with us. I didn't see any fun in it myself. Maybe I would have if I had been on the other end of the screaming and running.

We got our lantern back and my brother and his friend left. I was still mad but my friend Kyle didn't mind so much after he found out who it was.(Why would he mind? It wasn't his brother.) The next day I told my parents about it and they just smiled. You know, I wonder what being an only child is like.

Jeff Cavaness

THE GOATS

I've told you my family had all kinds of animals. What I ain't told you is that we didn't necessarily have all kinds of animals all the time. I remember the day we got the goats.

I was so excited. Everywhere I looked was pigs. I was ready for something different. Yes, having goats meant having more chores to do to help take care of them but I was glad to have something different.

How it came about was that a friend of my daddy's happen to ask him if he would like to have some goats. He wanted to git rid of his and he believed they would have a good home with us. My daddy said yes and then we started gitting a pen ready for them. One thing you need to know about goats is that "they ain't easy." First, we had to keep them away from the pigs. I don't know if that was for the pigs' or the goats' sake. Next, we took an old chicken house and pen, (My family used to sell eggs.), and remake it for goat use. Now, the goats we was gitting was tall goats. I don't remember what the breed was called. Actually, I don't even remember if'n I ever did know what kind of goats they were. I don't even know if'n my daddy knew.

We fixed fences and put up chicken wire on top of chicken wire thinking this would keep the goats from jumping over the fence. (It didn't work!) We converted the chicken coop for a shed for the goats and finally we were ready. At this point I was still excited. I couldn't wait.

The day came and my daddy's friend drove up with the goats. There was four of them. They were white and a couple of them had horns. They were baaing or bleating, whatever goats do. I knew they were ready to git out of the back of that truck. The man backed up the gate of the pen and opened the back of his truck and they jumped out. Looking back on that day now, I'm surprised they went in the pen so easily. I guess they were tired or scared from the trip. That was the last time they were easy.

You may have heard that goats like to eat anything and everything.

That's sorta true. Their pen was fair size. I don't think my daddy intended to keep them in that particular pen forever. I think he wanted to see how they would do and give them time to get used to their new surroundings.

(Surroundings is a good word. It's one of those words that make you sound you're smart.)

Apparently, those four goats got used to their

surroundings a little too good. Everyday there was some new problem. When I would git home from school there was always something I had to do with the goats. Then, the beginning of the end came to be. If there was one thing my daddy would get upset about with the animals was when they wouldn't stay in their pens.

That could git him so riled up I thought he would gotten rid of every animal on the place sometimes. The pen my daddy had worked so hard on for the goats was not good enough. Now, of course I didn't ever say it that way in front of him. Those goats were ornery and smart. They would find a weak spot in the wire or squeeze under or whatever it took to git out that pen. One week every day when the school bus would pull up to let me off the goats would be in the yard or not in sight at all.

It all ended the day the school bus had to stopped abruptly to avoid hitting one of the goats running across the road. The next day my daddy put them the back of his truck and took them to the sale barn in town and sold them. That was the first and last time we ever had goats. I always wondered if sheep would have been any easier. I don't think I'll ever find out. That's okay, if I ever want to look at a sheep, I'll find one somewheres else to look at.

Jeff Cavaness

LOVERS' LANE

Like all communities we had our legends about mysterious happenings. To be honest, I never experienced any unless you want to include Ol' Man Palmer and boy, did I ever experience him.

We had a couple of legends that was told around Hog Holler. One is about happenings on Lovers' Lane. Lovers' Lane was just a dirt (mostly dirt) and gravel road between us and town. I'm

Jeff Cavaness

sure that almost that almost every community in the United States have areas known as Lovers' Lane. I wonder if it's the same legend. (Probably not.)

The story surrounding Lovers' Lane concerns a man and woman who lived in town. They would go riding and always in up on Lovers' Lane. As I said, Lovers' Lane was just an old gravel road that connected our community to another one. It wasn't used much since the county had build a better road connection. That in itself is no big deal except that the woman's husband found this practice very irritating. Everyone around for miles knew what was going on but apparently it took the husband years to discover all the details. I don't know if the man's wife ever knew anything or not. (I didn't tell you the man was married too. I'm sorry.)

Well anyway, when the husband finally found out what was going on he started paying special attention to where his wife was going and who she was spending time with. Apparently, he discovered their meetings at Lovers' Lane. The way I hear it is that one night fairly soon after the man and woman had arrived at Lovers' Lane the husband sneaked up on them and shot them both dead and then shot himself. Now, the way I was told about the incident that it happened many years even before I was born. I don't know. I do know that the county decided that we didn't need Lover's Lane and let it grow up with weeds and brush so that no one could get down the road again. I passed this road every day on my way to school and you know, I never saw anyone on the road. I wonder if it was haunted. I think I do remember hearing somebody talk about hearing screams and shouts coming from there at night. Oh well, that's another story.

Jeff Cavaness

THE SCIENCE FAIR

When I was in the 10th grade, my Biology teacher, Mr. Williams, encouraged me to enter the Science Fair. Now, before I go any further, let me tell you about my science background. It was not much. I didn't particularly like science and I definitely did not have good science grades. I am not going out on a limb to say that science was probably my worst subject. I didn't like science and didn't specifically care about science.

That changed when I got into Biology class. I liked Mr. Williams and I liked Biology. It was interesting and at some times, even fascinating. I enjoyed that class for the most part and when Mr. Williams encouraged us to enter the Science Fair, I said why not.

The next problem was deciding what to do. I listened to other students discuss what they were going to do. Ideas ranged from building a working volcano or a working battery to drawing and charting the digestive system of the human body. I knew I couldn't compete with any of that. I thought and thought and got thoroughly frustrated. One day I was in the school library looking for ideas. I was in the science section and found a book on optical illusion. I opened and read some and looked at the pictures.

Hey! This is good. This stuff is interesting. I could do something with this.

I came to the conclusion that if I couldn't compete with scientific knowledge like the other students, I could compete with originality.

I started working. I studied optical illusions frontwards, backwards and everything in between. I am creative and I knew I had to use my own ideas and not someone else's. In my research and reading I discovered that the majority of the ideas that I heard my classmates discuss had already been done hundreds of times, may thousands of times. They were good ideas but I knew I had to do my own thing.

The day came when I had to bring my project to school to set up. I was so nervous. It fell apart in the car but somehow I got it up the third floor science lab and set it up. Some of the other students were there doing the same thing and they had some impressive displays. But I knew I did too.

Some of the students even made fun of mine. They were trying to get me to feel bad about my project. I knew I had a good project and would do well or so I prayed. The question would be if the judges would also think so.

Jeff Cavaness

That morning in Biology class Mr. Williams let us go tour the Science Fair and write down that we thought would win 1st, 2nd, and 3rd places. I'll be honest. I gave myself 3rd place. I knew I had worked hard and my project was impressive looking. Some of my friends teased me for thinking well of myself but I knew I had done well.

The plan was for the top winner to go to the District Science Fair. I didn't think too much about that. I just wanted to place in this Science Fair.

I couldn't think about anything else. Mr. Williams told us they would announce the winners that afternoon.

Sure enough, that afternoon during 6th period Algebra II class they asked for three students to report to the Chemistry Lab. My name was called our first. One of the other names called was Jason Holder. Jason was also in my class and we walked together toward the lab.

"Congratulations, Riley?"

"What do you mean?" I wasn't being modest. I knew I had won something but I was still counting on at least 3rd place.

"They called your name first. That means you won."

"Do you think so? I hope so."

We walked the rest of the way in silence. I was too excited to talk.

Could it be true? Could have truly won? Could I have beaten all those older and smarter students? Could I have won over all those more scientific projects?

We walked into the lab and Jason had been right. I had won. I got a check and a certificate and my picture in the paper. I couldn't believe it. I had won.

You know, all those wonderful ideas that those other students came up with, none of them won. All three projects that won had been totally original ideas. Mr. Williams told us that my winning had been unanimous among the four judges. They liked the originality of mine and the other two winners. I learned something that day. I learned that my ideas were ones to be proud of no matter what anyone else might say.

Jeff Cavaness

THE CHRISTMAS PLAY

I began writing stories when I was 13 years old. They were mostly silly little stories using characters like the ones I read about in other stories.

I was an early reader and loved to read. I still like to read. To me, the worst torture is not having a book handy to read at any given time. In fact, I've been known to have more than one book started at the same time. My wife likes to read and my little boy has loved books since before he even knew what one was.

Before I started writing, I used to tell myself stories. One aspect about growing up out in the country and with no one to play with, you learn how to entertain yourself. So many kids today can't do that. Heck, so many adults can't do that. My wife and I have worked hard in teaching and enabling our son to be able to entertain himself at least every once in a while. It is an uphill battle.

When I was in high school I wrote a couple of plays for our youth group at church to put on at church. One of the great things about being kin to most everyone in the church, you get to do what you want to do more times than not. One Christmas season our teacher told us that our class would be responsible for the Christmas program that year. I spoke up my ideas as usual.

"Mrs. Cotter, can we please do something different this year. I'm so tired of the same old Christmas pageant we do every year." (The

Hog Hollow

Cotters' was one of the few families at Standfield Chapel Presbyterian Church that wasn't kin to the Standfields'. I wonder if it was planned that way for her to be my Sunday School teacher.)

"Well, Riley, what do you suggest?"

I don't know if Mrs. Cotter was being sarcastic or not but I ignored her. (You know, sarcastic, doesn't look like it means, does it.)

"Mrs. Cotter, I just want to do something different. Something like we've never done before."

"Well, Riley, find me something."

I didn't find out until much later she was being sarcastic Well, being the kind of person I am I did go out and find something. I wrote a Christmas play. Now, this was not my first play to be done at church. The first one was when I was 13 or 14 years old. But this one was better. The next Sunday I marched up to Mrs. Cotter and gave her my play.

"Here you go, Mrs. Cotter, our Christmas play."

She looked at me for a moment. She looked a little confused. (I found out she never thought I would come up with anything so she had already ordered another play.)

"Okay, Riley. I'll read it and we'll go from there, okay."

"Sure, Mrs. Cotter, whatever you say."

I knew she would like it. Who wouldn't. The play was about two angels trying to find someone who knew the true meaning of Christmas.

After a few days Mrs. Cotter got in touch with me.

"Riley, I like your play. Let's get started."

Mrs. Cotter and the rest of the class helped but it was clear from early on that this play was my baby.

The play called for the angels to meet and talk to three people. They would show each person a scene from the first Christmas and in the background you would hear the choir singing a song that matched the scene.

We got great costumes. The scenery was

Hog Hollow

ready. I was so excited.

The night for the play came. The church was packed. It was the Sunday night before Christmas. This had always been a big night for the church and for Standfield Chapel. People who didn't ordinarily come to Standfield Chapel Presbyterian Church would come to the Christmas program. The cast was all excited and we started.

Everything went like clockwork. It was great! I was so happy until the second scene. This was the scene of when the wise men came to visit Baby Jesus. Of course, our camel was made of poster board and was tacked to the back wall. Each scene was completely different looking and each scene had to be changed as quick as possible. In the middle of this scene, the wise men are standing there and the choir is singing and suddenly the camel slowly starts falling to the floor. Looking back at the situation, the whole episode probably only lasted less than five seconds. But then, it felt as if it lasted for an hour. You know though, the actors and the choir went on as if nothing had happened and we finished the play without a hitch. The congregation loved it and I was congratulated many, many times.

I learned something though. As much as I loved doing the play and seeing it come to life, my biggest thrill was that there was people hearing my words and sharing in my vision. That is something I have never forgotten and is probably one of the reasons you are reading this.

THE PIG FARMER AND THE DEBUTANTE

Actually, the title of this tale should be "The Pig Farmer's Son and the Debutante". Because I wasn't actually the pig farmer but I was his son.

Do you know what a debutante is? I did but I never thought I would meet one while living on the farm. I was right, I didn't meet Joy until I was grown and had moved away from the farm and

Jeff Cavaness

from Standfield Chapel.

The dictionary says a "debutante" is a young lady is making her first appearances in a formal social function. Since I never had ever been to a social function, formal or otherwise, I believed I was pretty safe in assuming I would never meet a debutante.

I was wrong. I met Joy a few years after I completed college. She had moved to the town I lived in and we met through mutual friends. It was love at first sight for both of us. We had a whirlwind courtship and a wonderful wedding followed. That was twelve years ago and I have been eternally thankful to God ever since.

Now, to be honest, I didn't know Joy was a debutante when I met her and I didn't know until we were engaged to be married that I found out. I found out by accident. Joy had never been impressed about being a debutante. She had gone through with it only because her mother and grandmother had wanted her to. She went through with it with the same attitude she handles most things in life. She approached the experience as something to enjoy and learn from. She told me that at the Debutante Ball she and another girl had on the same white dress. Joy had gotten hers in one city and the other girl in another. Joy told her that apparently they both had great taste in clothes. The other girl was mortified seeing another girl with her dress on and burst into tears and ran off. (I hope I never get that attached to anything I have on!)

But I'm ahead of myself again. Let me explain to all you country folk, like me, who don't know what being a debutante means. It means that at a Debutante Ball (dance) a young lady is presented to society. Her father or other male figure escorts her. All the girls wear white dresses and it is the "social event of the season."

I was surprised that stuff still happened in today's world but let me tell you, apparently, some people take it very serio usly. Joy, on the otherhand, just thought it was silly and was glad when it was over. But I still got me a debutante

Jeff Cavaness

for a wife and I couldn't be happier. I would recommend it to anyone if they can find someone like my Joy.

SURPRISE! I'M A FARM BOY

During part of my professional working time I was a high school English Teacher. It was funny being called Mr. Standfield by the students. I was the first one in my family to go to college and complete my studies. Today, I have achieved my Masters' Degree. That I got for myself.

Anyway, in English class a teacher tries to impart language skills to their students that will help them in life. As I learned most students don't give a flip about English and language skills. My first years teaching was in a very rural part of the state. Most of my students would never go to college and of those who did, at least half would not finish. They would remain on the farm or work in factories. They mostly didn't see the need for proper English speaking and especially on paper. I tried to explain the need but my first year I hit on sure fire way to get their attention and I still use this shocker.

"Class, let me tell you why I know that most of you will need to know how to use proper English in your speaking and on paper."

"How many of you plan on going to college?"

A few students would raise their hands.

"Okay, we know you need to have good English language skills. Now, how many of you plan on farming?"

More students would raise their hands.

"Okay, how many of you plan on buying land, houses, cars, and farm equipment?"

Hog Hollow

Most of the class would raise their hands.

"Don't you think that when you sit in front of the loan officer or try to complete a loan application, you might like to know how to do it using good English so you don't sound like you are from the back side of Podunk?"

(Podunk is my imaginary town where all hicks are from.)

The students start to mumble among themselves and usually at least one will ask me a question.

"Mr. Standfield, how do you know about loan applications and farm equipment. You went to college."

"Because I grew up on a farm and a pig farm at that."

I usually give them a moment to digest that surprise and then continue.

"Yes, I'm a farm boy and I remember my daddy sitting at the kitchen table trying to figure out how to complete a loan application. And I remember how difficult it was at times for him and my mother and their dropout education." (Actually, my mother did get her GED and took some college courses later in her life after my brother and I were older.)

Usually my students would at least act a little more interested in what I was saying. Of course, the farm kids wanted to know about my childhood and what I did and had done and how many pigs and cows and what crops. The point was that I got their attention and maybe, just maybe, they paid a little more attention to English at least for a few days.

MEMORIES OF THE FARM

You've been reading about my memories of growing up on the farm. Those memories have taken the shape of short stories but other memories are the ones I want to share with you now. These memories are just thoughts and incidents frozen in time for me and you too, I hope.

Seeing all the baby animals on the farm.

Being quiet in the woods and seeing deer

feeding and passing by. Gathering around a bonfire and telling ghost stories and eating hotdogs until we popped.

Knowing that everyone in the neighborhood is safe and you don't have to check your Halloween candy.

Sliding on a frozen pond or creek.

Playing in the leaves in the fall.

Swinging on wild grape vines in the woods.

Exploring creeks and gulleys and playing like you find buried treasure. (I actually did find parts of an old moonshine still one. It was old and rusted but it was definitely a still.)

Walking across a pasture at night with the air so clear and so many stars you feel like you can just reach up and grab one.

Riding horses.

Going on hayrides.

Playing hide and seek in the barn loft.

Making homemade ice cream and taking turns turning the crank.

Picking blackberries and eating more than you

put in the bucket.

Catching fireflys and watching them light up a jar. (Always let them out before you go to bed or they die.)

Lying in bed with the bedroom window open and listening to all the night sounds.

Having a friend sleep over and staying up late.

Climbing apple trees and picking apples to eat and take home.

Climbing trees and seeing how high I could get without falling and breaking my neck.

Eating watermelon on my uncle's back porch. He had the best watermelons I have ever eaten to this day. He said it was because he used mule manure for fertilizer. He probably did. Whatever he used, they were great watermelons.

Playing in the woods after a big snow.

Having a tire swing. (For all those of you who do not know what that is – it is a swing made out of an old car tire.)

Climbing the cherry tree to get to the cherries

before the birds got them.

Playing in the cotton trailer during cotton picking time.

Just playing in the dirt.

Naming the farm animals.

Going with your parents to the sale barn watching how well your animals sell.

Sledding down the hill while dodging trees.

Making a tent out of quilts in the living room and sleeping on the floor that night.

Seeing how high you can get on the front porch swing.

Taking old scraps of wood and building anything.

Creating little worlds in the pig lot and watching the pigs tear them up.

Trying to figure out just how many different things a hog will actually eat.

Having puppies knock you down and crawl all over you trying to lick your face.

Finding a 'possum with babies in the bottom of the dog feed barrel.

Having picnics with family and friends.

Sitting out under the shade tree drinking lemonade and waving to the cars as they go by.

Most of all, taking pride in the fact that you are making a difference.

Jeff Cavaness

HOG HOLLER REVISITED

I hope you have enjoyed the stories about my growing up in Hog

Holler. As you can see I have included some stories concerning my adult years. This collection came about because one night my son wanted me to tell him a bedtime story and I started telling him about my childhood. His particular favorites were always about the farm animals. His extra special story was the one about the goose.

As I told him the stories I decided that I needed to write these stories down for him and his children. One aspect of my life you may have picked up was that I have never gone back to Hog Holler to live. I have chosen a more cosmopolitan lifestyle and don't regret that decision at all. The only regrets I have, if indeed I have any, is that my son will never truly understand the kind of childhood his daddy had. He has seen where I grew up and he has listened to my stories but since he is basically a city kid, he doesn't really understand.

There are many parts of my upbringing that I'm very proud, especially the values I learned along the way. After living in at least three major American cities, I believe their lifestyles are too fast-paced for some of the simple joys and times I experienced. Don't get me wrong, I'm not saying children raised in towns and cities don't have any values. I'm just saying that I believe a simpler lifestyle is more preferable for teaching and learning basic good living values. In the country, even with computers, people do not have as many influences and pulls on their time.

I can remember running and playing through the woods and pastures.

I can remember all types of animals being around to look at and play with. I can also remember having to take care of all those animals. I remember when my wife and I got our son his first pet, two puppies. They were cute and a lot of fun and my son just loved having them. But I hate to admit that one of the first thoughts concerning the dogs was all the care they needed and would need. I'm glad we got them but I am very thankful I don't have 500 pigs to take care of too.

ABOUT THE AUTHOR

Jeff Cavaness writes and lives in Middleton, Tennessee with his wife, Jane, and their son, Adam. Middleton is located in the southwestern corner of the state. He is currently a Guidance Counselor at the local high school.

Like the character, Riley, Jeff too grew up on a pig farm and lived in a community similar to Hog Hollow. He left the farm to study education at The University of Tennessee at Martin. He later returned to receive his Masters' Degree in

Educational Psychology.

Jeff has enjoyed reading all his life and his favorite stories are those that depict everyday happenings with real characters. This book came about because of his son Adam asking for a bedtime story about Jeff growing up on the farm.

While telling the story a thought came to Jeff, "I should write this stuff down for my son to have one day".

Jeff continues to write and is in the process of completing a second book continuing the life of Riley Washington Standfield.

Printed in the United States
27369LVS00001B/76-90